Ride the Savage River

It took Marshal Ellis Moore twelve years to clean up Empire Falls, and he was killed taking on the last of the gun-toters who had controlled his town. But at his funeral US Marshal Lincoln Hawk told his sons Daniel and Henry that all was not as it seems. Ellis had been on the payroll of Samuel Holdstock, who controlled Skull Bend from his steamboat, and who was now spreading his corrupting influence down-river.

Daniel and Henry vowed to expose the full truth. To do that they would need to infiltrate Samuel's domain, spirit him away from his steamboat, and then deliver him to justice in Empire Falls. Even the formidable Lincoln Hawk reckoned their mission was doomed to fail, but to put right their father's mistakes they would have to succeed.

By the same author

Ambush in Dust Creek
Silver Gulch Feud
Blood Gold
Golden Sundown
Clearwater Justice
Hellfire
Escape from Fort Benton
Return to Black Rock
The Man They Couldn't Hang
Last Stage to Lonesome
McGuire, Manhunter
Raiders of the Mission San Juan
Coltaine's Revenge
Stand-Off at Copper Town
Siege at Hope Wells
The Sons of Casey O'Donnell

Ride the Savage River

Scott Connor

A Black Horse Western

ROBERT HALE · LONDON

ISBN 978-0-7090-9350-3

Robert Hale Limited
Clerkenwell House
Clerkenwell Green
London EC1R 0HT

www.halebooks.com

Typeset by
Derek Doyle & Associates, Shaw Heath
Printed and bound in Great Britain by
CPI Antony Rowe, Chippenham and Eastbourne

CHAPTER 1

'Is he dead?' Daniel Moore asked.

Marshal Ellis Moore knelt beside the prone form of Jed Shaw and felt his neck.

'No,' he said. 'He's only been beaten.'

He got confirmation that he'd been right when Jed stirred and then groaned. With Daniel taking one arm and Ellis the other, they dragged him to the side of the alley and propped him up against the wall.

'Who?' Daniel asked, kneeling down to look him in the eye.

Ellis uttered a harsh laugh and, despite the low light level, which masked most of his features, Daniel saw his narrowed-eyed glare that said they all knew the answer to this question.

'Mitch Casey,' Jed said. He fingered the oozing scrape on his cheek and winced. 'I ignored the Barker brothers' last warning.'

Ellis patted Jed's shoulder.

'In which case,' he said, 'they've had their last warning too.'

He glanced at Daniel and jerked his head to the side, silently ordering him to leave with him, but Daniel leaned in towards Jed.

'For the record,' he said, 'what was that last warning?'

Before he could answer, Ellis snorted.

'Forgive my son,' he said, shaking his head. 'Since I appointed him as my deputy he's had these strange notions about keeping records.'

'That's all right,' Jed said managing a smile. 'They said I shouldn't gamble in the Lucky Star saloon no more or Mitch would deal with me. I didn't gamble, but I did go in there for a drink.'

Ellis looked at Daniel. 'That enough for you, son?'

'It is, Marshal,' Daniel said. 'We had to make sure before we took them on.'

With that matter concluded, Daniel got to his feet and joined Ellis. After checking that Jed was fit enough to be left alone, side by side the two lawmen headed down the road towards the Barker brothers' saloon.

'What would have happened,' Ellis said, 'if I'd spent the last twelve years standing around making sure?'

Daniel smiled, enjoying seeing his father being enthused and in control again.

The last few months had been tough. The old

marshal had three weeks left to serve of what he had promised would be his final term, but there had been times recently when Daniel had been unsure if he would see those days out.

Not that Ellis would talk about his illness. He didn't let Daniel or his other son, Henry, join him when he saw Doc Taylor. Any questions about the all-too-obvious signs of whatever was eating him up inside were met with the stubbornness that had helped to make him into the formidable man he had once been.

'You'd never have cleaned up Empire Falls,' Daniel said. Then, as they approached the saloon, he quietened to consider the task ahead.

The brothers had arrived eight years ago and set themselves up as the main competition to Wesley Truscott's Riverview Saloon. Unlike the larger saloon, their establishment attracted trouble but, as Ellis had plenty of other problems to deal with, he hadn't worried about them until now.

'Take the back door,' Ellis said, pointing. 'It's always open. Go in and wait outside the saloon room until you hear me come in. Then. . . .'

Daniel continued nodding while he waited for his father to complete his orders.

'Then what?' he prompted.

He didn't get an answer, so he turned just as Ellis keeled over. Daniel grabbed his shoulders and, with a firm grip, he stopped him from dropping to the ground.

7

'Let me sit down,' Ellis croaked, his voice sounding older than his years.

Daniel helped him to sit on the edge of the boardwalk outside the bank, where Ellis held his head in his hands, gasping in air. After a minute, with a determined breath, he sat up straight. He spat on the hardpan and, in the low light, Daniel was sure the moisture was tinged with red before it soaked into the dirt.

'We don't need to do this tonight,' Daniel said. 'We can—'

'It's tonight or never,' Ellis snapped.

'You're not that ill,' Daniel said.

Ellis cast him a long look and for a moment Daniel thought he might confide in him, but he gave a wan smile instead.

'We'll talk properly later, but these are the last snakes to spear before I can claim I made Empire Falls a place fit for decent folk to raise a family.' He patted Daniel's shoulder. 'Will you help me?'

'Sure,' Daniel said, helping him to his feet.

Ellis looked at him with his head cocked on one side, looking as if he wanted to say something more. Then he waved at him to leave.

A wide gap between the Lucky Star saloon and the next building, courtesy of a never-explained fire two years ago, let Daniel remain in the light when he skirted around the saloon, but the back was shrouded in darkness.

Before he disappeared around the corner he

glanced into the road. His father was standing at the other corner, waiting for him to get into position.

Daniel gave him a thumbs-up signal. Then, with care he picked his way through the darkness to reach the back door. When he heard no sounds coming from within, he put a hand to the wood and pushed.

The door didn't move, and neither did it open when he pushed it more firmly with a shoulder. The rattling sound and the door's solid feeling gave the impression that it had been barred.

He stood back, wondering what had gone wrong. His father had been sure the door would be open and it wasn't like him to make such a basic mistake. His body was weakening, not his mind.

A gunshot tore out from within the saloon, closely followed by a second shot. Angry voices made demands, one of them his father's. Then a volley of rapid shots echoed.

With all chance of sneaking inside gone, he kicked the door. When it failed to move, he kicked it again, this time with his heart sinking in frustration.

Then he winced. His father had known the door was barred. He'd known he'd be safe here while he took on the Barker brothers single handed.

He slapped the door in anger and then broke into a run. He rounded the first corner at a sprint, only slowing after he'd turned the second corner and reached the window. After the initial gunfire, the shooting hadn't continued, but he heard raised voices.

From a side-on position he couldn't see the bar, but he could see his father standing a few paces in from the doorway, his gun drawn and aimed at someone who was out of his view.

Since the situation appeared to have gone well he edged forward and saw that the Barker brothers were both standing with their hands raised. The prone form of their hired thug, Mitch Casey, lay at their feet, a thin stream of blood spreading out from under his form.

Sure now about what he'd face, he walked past the window. With his gun drawn, he pushed through the batwings to stand alongside his father.

'You took your time,' Ellis said from the corner of his mouth.

'I had to deal with a closed door,' Daniel said.

'Then that gave you a tougher fight than these varmints put up.' Ellis gestured with his gun to indicate the door. 'You'll go outside first.'

By the bar the brothers looked at each other with surly confidence.

'What you trying to do, Marshal?' Trent, the elder brother, said. 'We're law-abiding men and Sheridan will clear up this little misunderstanding.'

'He can try.' Ellis smiled. 'But he'll explain from the cell beside yours.'

Trent's right eye twitched with concern. Sheridan was the brothers' lawyer who had always been on hand to explain away problems.

The younger brother, Maxwell, stepped forward.

'You'd better hope you can see this through. You've made some powerful enemies tonight.'

'I've got some powerful friends.'

'We know, but we never thought you'd have the guts to use them.'

Ellis gestured at the door again, this time with greater vehemence.

'Save your breath. Your whining don't interest me.'

Daniel caught an odd change in Ellis's tone. He hadn't been sure what Maxwell had meant with his comment about powerful friends, and he looked at his father to see how he was reacting.

What he saw worried him. Sweat was running from the older man's brow and he was grinding his jaw, using the steady chewing motion he always used when he was in pain but he was trying to avoid showing it.

Daniel stepped forward. 'I can take care of these two. You get Sheridan.'

Ellis gave a grateful nod, but the comment made Maxwell smirk.

'We can save you the trouble,' he said.

For several seconds silence reigned until Daniel saw Maxwell's telltale eye-flicker. Daniel glanced to the side to see that Sheridan was coming in through the doorway to the back room, the way Daniel would have used if the door hadn't been barred.

11

A demand was on Daniel's lips for Sheridan to raise his hands, but he didn't get the time to utter it before Sheridan stepped forward. To Daniel's surprise he was brandishing a six-shooter. Before Daniel could turn his gun on him, Sheridan fired, his shot tearing into Ellis's side and making him stumble and then double over.

Daniel made him pay for his sneaky act. He slammed lead into the lawyer's chest making him spin round into the doorjamb where he stood propped up for a moment, then keeled over.

Before he'd hit the floor, Maxwell scrambled for his gun, but as he touched leather Daniel dispatched him with a high shot to the shoulder that sent him staggering backwards into the bar. A second shot to the guts made him fold and then fall.

Trent took flight and, with a lithe motion, he slapped a hand on the bar and vaulted it. Daniel's quick shot tore splinters from the bar before he disappeared from view.

Daniel stood poised, waiting to see if he'd immediately spring back up, but when he didn't, he grabbed Ellis's right shoulder and moved to direct him to the back of the saloon where he could sit.

Ellis grunted and threw him off.

'It's not supposed to end this way,' he muttered.

'Just rest,' Daniel said, again trying to move him, but with a great roar Ellis lashed out and forced him away.

Blood soaked his vest, but that didn't stop him

12

standing upright. He raised a hand and, thinking he was now requesting help, Daniel moved in. But then he found that Ellis had bunched a fist. With a backward swipe of the hand, he punched his cheek and sent him to the floor.

Daniel landed on his back. As he shook himself, feeling more shocked than hurt, Ellis staggered away with his gun thrust out. He made four lurching paces and then bellied up to the bar.

A grin broke his grim visage as Trent bobbed up and swung his gun round. Simultaneous gunshots tore out. Ellis's shot sent Trent staggering backwards into the mirror behind the bar where, with a wild shake of his arms, he cracked the glass and then fell over.

Ellis staggered sideways. He moved to grab the bar to stop himself falling, but he failed and tumbled over to lie on his side.

Despite seeing his father fall, Daniel jumped to his feet and ran his gaze over the two visible fallen men, confirming they were still. Then he hurried to the bar. Only when he'd seen that Trent had been killed did he kneel beside his father.

'You shouldn't have done that,' he said.

'I should,' Ellis murmured, his voice fading fast. 'That was the way it was supposed to end.'

'For you, perhaps, but it's not what I wanted.' Daniel cradled him against his chest.

'Always think kindly of me,' Ellis breathed, his eyes now unfocused.

'I will,' Daniel said. 'The whole town will cheer when they hear what you did tonight and there's no way. . . .'

Daniel trailed off. He was speaking to himself.

CHAPTER 2

'It looks as if everyone in town has turned out to say goodbye,' Wesley Truscott said.

Daniel considered the rows of people flanking the road on the way to the Riverview Saloon. He judged that Wesley was right; that the whole town wanted to share memories of the man who had tamed Empire Falls.

'So they should,' Daniel said. 'They owe him a lot.'

'We all do, and that's why I'd be obliged if you'd tell your brother not to insult me by offering to pay for today.'

Daniel hadn't meant his comment to be taken that way, but he nodded. He'd already offered to pay, but persuading Sergeant Henry Moore would be a different matter.

Henry was the elder brother and his rapid promotion through the ranks at Fort Lord now meant he took a dim view of anyone who didn't agree with him.

The fact that neither of them could afford to feed an entire town wouldn't concern him.

Presently they both faced the front when the open wagon carrying Marshal Ellis Moore's coffin made its slow way down the road. Ellis had served for twenty years in the military before he'd settled in Empire Falls to become the town marshal, and he had retained links with Fort Lord.

So Henry rode up front while an honour guard of four troopers rode along behind. Henry relaxed his stiff-backed stance to give Daniel a smile that acknowledged they would both be happier once the formalities were over.

Outside the wide door to the saloon, Henry drew up. Then, with the four troopers each taking a corner of the coffin, they paraded inside. Only when they'd moved out of sight did people mill in, although they left space for Daniel and Henry to stand on either side of the door, where they welcomed everyone as they entered.

Wesley was the first to go in, giving each man a nod. Then the rest of the townsfolk moved closer.

Only a quarter of the people who passed by could fit inside, but the Riverview Saloon made good use of its location. Large doors on the other side led out on to a wooden pier where everyone could stand.

As they passed, the mourners said a few words. Some dallied to offer a personal platitude or to relate a fondly remembered incident about Ellis.

Over the next half-hour Daniel confirmed why

the town had stopped their business today to pay their respects. Many owed their lives to Ellis, and they all knew the town was peaceful only because of him.

By the time the last few people were slipping by, even the usually taciturn Henry had had to wipe his eyes several times. He caught Daniel's eye and, now that there were only stragglers left, he moved over to join him.

'I knew this would be a tough day,' he said, 'but these tales help.'

'Everyone cares,' Daniel said. 'In the end that's all that matters.'

Henry nodded. 'I hope this is the way he wanted to be remembered.'

Henry gave Daniel a significant look, and catching his meaning Daniel nodded. Since Henry had been serving at Fort Lord he had been home for only rare visits recently.

'He often got sick the last few weeks. He wouldn't talk about it, but I'm sure he dreaded a lingering end. I'd prefer to have him around still, but I reckon that when I look back, I'll accept this way was better.'

'He finished the job.' Henry smiled. 'That means the new marshal will have an easy time.'

Daniel returned the smile. The subject of who would now become town marshal hadn't been discussed that he knew of but, despite his limited experience, Daniel hoped the mayor would give him a chance. He was unsure if it was appropriate to mention it today, but he would be sure to talk to him later.

With that in mind he tipped his hat to the last two mourners and then moved to follow them inside. But Henry raised a hand to stop him and drew his attention to a man who was standing at the back of the wagon that had carried the coffin.

He was looking at the wagon while clearly being deep in thought. Daniel didn't recognize him.

'Let's get the last one in,' Daniel said.

Henry nodded. The two men headed over to him.

'I don't know you,' Henry said, 'but we're obliged you've come to pay your respects. You're welcome to come in and have a drink to Ellis's memory.'

The man continued to look at the wagon as if he were finishing his thoughts. Then he turned and fixed Henry and then Daniel with his piercing gaze.

He was bearded, younger than Ellis had been, and he wore the star of a US marshal.

'You'd be Ellis's?' he asked.

'We are.' Daniel raised his eyebrows, requesting a name.

'Marshal Lincoln Hawk.' He looked around. 'I rode with your father when he left the cavalry and became a lawman.'

Daniel nodded. Ellis hadn't moved his family here until he'd defeated the worst of the gun-slingers, so he hadn't met Lincoln before, but he had heard of him.

'Then we'd welcome hearing stories of those days.'

'I don't tell stories.'

Lincoln turned to leave, but Daniel moved to block his way.

'Then don't say anything. But I'm sure my father would have wanted you to be here.'

Lincoln looked Daniel up and down, his flared eyes and bunched fists suggesting that despite the situation, he was ready to bat him aside.

'I'm sure he would,' he snapped. 'Now get out of my way or, son or no son of Ellis Moore, I'll move you aside.'

Lincoln's anger surprised Daniel, so he stayed rooted to the spot.

'I don't know what's worrying you.'

Lincoln took a long pace to stand toe to toe with Daniel, forcing him to lean backwards.

'I knew your father when he was a lawman who knew his own mind, but then he got his influential friends.' Lincoln pointed at the Riverview Saloon with a brisk gesture that clipped Daniel's shoulder. It was only a glancing blow, but it sent him to his knees. Lincoln loomed over him. 'I'd prefer to remember him the way he was before it all happened.'

Lincoln took a long pace over Daniel's supine form. A heel clipped his hip, but that didn't slow him.

'His illness wasn't his fault,' Daniel shouted.

Lincoln stomped to a halt, stood for a moment, then continued walking. Daniel got to his feet and moved to go after him while demanding to know what he meant, but Henry hurried on and slapped an arm across his chest.

'Leave him,' he said, directing him to go to the saloon.

'But what did he mean?'

Lincoln had now reached the horse he'd tethered outside the bank. Without looking at them, he mounted up and headed away.

'I'm sure it was nothing to worry about.' Henry's strained tone suggested he wasn't taking his own advice. 'Perhaps they argued.'

'Possibly, but he said that Pa had influential friends, and Maxwell Barker said something like that before Pa died.'

Daniel waited for Henry to offer an opinion, but when he couldn't, they both shrugged. Together they headed into the saloon.

For the next hour, as he reminisced with Ellis's old friends, Daniel tried to avoid dwelling on the odd encounter, but whenever there was a lull, he couldn't help but ponder on Lincoln's comment. He didn't reach any firm conclusions.

It was late afternoon when he found himself standing in a group with Mayor Glover. After a few minutes of friendly chatter, Glover took him by the arm and manoeuvred him outside to a quiet spot.

'I assume,' he said without preamble when they

were alone, 'you wish to continue your father's good work?'

'I'd like to serve as town marshal,' Daniel said, 'but I won't put pressure on you to make a decision, and especially not today.'

'I know, and so rest easy. I won't decide for several days, but it looks as if it'll be choice between you and a new man, Ronald Kearny. He rode in today with a strong recommendation.'

'From Marshal Lincoln Hawk?' Daniel said.

Glover flinched back in surprise.

'How did you know that? That information is supposed to be known only by Lincoln and myself.'

'A good lawman always knows what's going on,' Daniel said glibly, although his mind was whirling as he tried to piece together what he thought might be happening.

Glover gave him an odd look, but he didn't press the matter. Even so, when Daniel resumed walking around the gathering, he couldn't help but listen out for any mention of Ronald Kearny. He didn't hear anyone speak about him.

It was approaching sundown, the time they had allotted for the private burial attended by just himself, Henry and his father's closest friends when his neck burned with a familiar feeling of being watched.

From the corner of his eye he looked at the bar. A man he didn't recognize was looking at him and he didn't look away.

With Henry trying to catch his eye to say that they needed to leave, Daniel didn't feel in the mood to talk to him yet. So he limited himself to going over to the bar to stand beside him.

'Later, Ronald,' he said simply.

'Later,' Ronald said, acknowledging that he had guessed his name correctly with a wink, 'when your important friends aren't around.'

Daniel firmed his jaw to avoid reacting. He turned his back on Ronald and joined his brother in carrying out the last, sad duty of the day.

CHAPTER 3

'What's on your mind?' Daniel said, standing in the doorway to Ronald Kearny's hotel room.

Ronald was sitting by the window and he gestured to the chair on the other side of the window.

'Rest,' he said, smiling. 'You've had a tough day.'

Daniel refused to let Ronald's pleasant mood lighten his own sour mood, although he sat. For the last hour, even as the troopers had lowered his father into the ground, he had dwelt on Lincoln's antipathy and the comments others had made about Ellis's friends.

'I did, and that wasn't made easier by you and Marshal Lincoln Hawk. While saying goodbye I shouldn't have to deal with that.'

'I'm sorry you're annoyed, but a clean sweep is required.' Ronald glanced out of the window to look at the law office. 'That's what Lincoln thought fifteen years ago when he recommended your father for the position.'

Daniel sighed, now even more bemused.

'Then why did he not even want to pay his respects?'

'He did, in his own way. Lincoln is a tough man and he's not a hypocrite. He wouldn't step foot in a saloon owned by Wesley Truscott, unless it was with a gun drawn and an arrest warrant in his pocket.'

Daniel nodded. 'So the important friends that worried you and Lincoln include Wesley?'

'They do.' Ronald spread his hands and offered a placating smile. 'But we can speak of this another day when you—'

'We'll speak of it now,' Daniel snapped waving an arm in irritation. He jumped to his feet. 'I've had enough of the snide comments about my father. He's in the ground now, so if you have something to say, say it.'

Ronald looked up at him calmly, but he said nothing until Daniel sat down again.

'It'll be better for Empire Falls if I become the town marshal,' he said levelly. 'I don't want to make this hard for you, but if you insist, I'll reveal why. On the other hand, if you step aside, I'll get the job done without embarrassing you and without tarnishing the memory of a man who did much good for Empire Falls.'

'Stop speaking in riddles.'

Ronald considered him, his grinding jaw conveying that he was wondering whether to reply.

'Marshal Ellis Moore was on the payroll of a corrupt man. He may have devoted his time to cleaning up Empire Falls, but he only took on those who opposed the man he worked for. Whether you're involved in that or not, the town doesn't need another Moore as a lawman. I'm on nobody's payroll and I'll finish the job your father might have completed before his unfortunate demise, both physically and morally.'

Daniel stared at Ronald agog.

'I don't believe that,' he murmured.

'Your expression says this is news to you. So I'm sorry you had to hear it, but I hope that once you've considered, you'll step aside.'

'The name,' Daniel muttered, finally letting his anger get the better of him. He leapt out of his chair and rocked forward to loom over Ronald. 'Tell me who you claim was paying my father.'

'The same man who bankrolls Wesley Truscott,' Ronald said, still appearing calm and unconcerned despite Daniel's outburst. 'Samuel Holdstock.'

'Nothing,' Daniel snapped, throwing the last bundle of clothing to the floor.

'I never expected there would be,' Henry said, surveying the mess with a horrified expression that only a man who lived an ordered life could assume.

Daniel kicked a pile of discarded clothes aside.

'Then why did Ronald say those things?'

Henry went to his knees to pick up the scattered clothing. Then he moved off to gather up the rest of the belongings that Daniel had strewn in his wake while searching for the bribes his father had apparently received.

Ellis had lived a frugal life. His home on the edge of town was close to the Riverview Saloon, but it had none of the grandeur of that imposing establishment.

Aside from enjoying a whiskey late at night when he was off duty, Ellis had rarely spent money on anything other than essentials. He refused to gamble and the few clothes Daniel had rummaged through represented the sum total of his possessions. If ever there was a man who looked as if he'd never taken a bribe, it was his father.

The only explanation Daniel had considered was that he had hated himself for taking money and so he had stored it away somewhere, but, if he had, Daniel couldn't find it.

'Daniel,' Henry said at last, 'have you considered the simpler explanation? Ronald Kearny wants your job.'

Daniel started to shake his head, but then he snorted and spread his hands.

'I hadn't, but that still doesn't feel likely. For that US marshal to have taken an interest there must be some substance behind these allegations.'

'Substance isn't proof.'

'It isn't, but allegations can destroy a man's good name as much as proof can. If I stand aside and let Ronald become town marshal, he'll keep those allegations secret. If I don't, he'll tell everyone.'

'That sounds like blackmail to me.'

Daniel frowned. 'It does. So what do I do?'

Henry rubbed his trim moustache before he answered.

'I have to be back at the fort by noon tomorrow. So you'll have to do what you think is best.'

'Obliged for your confidence in me.' Daniel joined Henry in picking up clothes. 'But I don't even know where to start.'

Henry straightened up, his jutting jaw showing that even if he couldn't help, he was determined to be useful.

'Perhaps the answer lies with the man who apparently knew our father better than we did.'

Nightfall was approaching and Marshal Lincoln Hawk had settled down for the night.

His horse was idly chewing leaves from a dangling branch; a rolled-up blanket and saddle lay propped up against a boulder. But the camp itself was deserted, as the lawman was lying on his chest in the undergrowth.

Presently, the man who had been following him approached the camp. He called out for permission to enter. Lincoln recognized the voice, but he didn't respond, so his pursuer dismounted.

'Lincoln,' Daniel Moore said, pacing closer to the fire and now sounding worried, 'are you here?'

Lincoln waited until Daniel had walked round the fire and had taken a few paces past him. Then he got to his feet and silently stalked up to him from behind.

A crunched footfall alerted Daniel a moment before Lincoln slapped a rough hand around his chin. Then Lincoln held him firm while thrusting cold steel against his neck.

'Make one wrong move, Ellis Moore's son,' he muttered in his ear, 'and it'll be your last.'

'I didn't come to cause no trouble,' Daniel said. 'I want to talk to you about my father.'

'I said everything I needed to in Empire Falls.'

Lincoln gripped his chin more tightly, but then, with a muttered grunt, he tipped Daniel's six-shooter from its holster and shoved him forward to make him go sprawling.

Daniel hit the ground and slid towards the fire. Then he had to dig in his elbows and scramble to the side to avoid the flames. On his back, he looked up at Lincoln and faced his drawn gun.

'Then,' Daniel murmured with a resigned shrug, 'I'd like to hear about the good times you had with him.'

'We had no good times.' Lincoln snorted. 'We just lived when others didn't.'

Despite his unpromising comment, Daniel moved over to sit on the other side of the fire.

Lincoln lowered his gun, although he didn't holster it.

'I can see you don't want to talk, but at least tell me how it went wrong for my father.'

'Ask Ronald Kearny.'

'I did, but he wasn't helpful. I reckon he didn't know much.'

Lincoln smiled, acknowledging that for the first time Daniel had made a perceptive comment. He holstered his gun.

'Sometimes not knowing the full facts keeps your mind clear to do the right thing. That's what Ellis did when he first went to Empire Falls.'

'And now the town's peaceful and filled with decent folk attracted to the safe environment he created.'

Lincoln leaned forward. 'It's safe for some, but just because you don't see who's suffering, it doesn't mean it's not happening.'

'And that's Samuel Holdstock's fault?'

'So Ronald does know some details.' Lincoln rubbed his jaw. 'Samuel owns Wesley Truscott. Everything Wesley earns, he takes a cut to build his empire.'

Daniel looked north. 'In Skull Bend?'

Lincoln nodded. 'Samuel owns that town, every building, every man. Even the town marshal Cliff Stroud is his right-hand man. But one day that won't be enough and he'll move in on Empire Falls. Your father worked for him, so what will his reputation be

29

like then?'

'If that happens, it'll be bad for everyone, but then again I've seen no sign of these bribes he was supposed to have taken.'

'Not all bribes involve money changing hands; sometimes they repay a debt.'

Daniel winced and lowered his head.

'How did he get into debt?'

'The usual way, gambling.'

'My father didn't gamble.'

'Why do you think he gave it up?' Lincoln rolled forward to kneel. He poked at the fire. 'When Samuel was starting out he targeted your father. He gave him leeway to build a small debt into a large one. Then he called it in and the price was to leave Wesley alone.'

Daniel gnawed his bottom lip as he considered.

'I don't know what to believe, but I figure there's only one way I can put this right. I'll bring Samuel Holdstock to justice, with your help.'

Lincoln paused from tending the fire to raise an eyebrow.

'You won't get it . . . yet. I'm on the trail of a former associate of Samuel, the bank robber Adna Burroughs. He's the nearest I or anyone else will get to Samuel right now. I'll settle for bringing Adna to justice. Then one day I'll take down Marshal Stroud, and then, last of all, Samuel.'

Daniel snorted. 'If taking on Samuel directly is too tough for you, I'll do it alone.'

Lincoln chuckled. 'You've got some of your father in you. I hope it's the better part.' He considered Daniel. 'So what's your plan?'

'I haven't got one, but I'll think of something on the way.'

Lincoln waved a hand as he struggled to voice how ill-conceived an idea this was.

'And you're just going to ride into a town Samuel owns on your own and take him on, are you?'

Daniel opened his mouth to reply, but he said nothing as Lincoln then ripped his gun from its holster. As the gun swung up, Daniel flinched away, his wide-eyed expression registering shock. But Daniel wasn't Lincoln's target.

Someone was creeping about in the undergrowth.

Long moments passed with Daniel staying crouched down and Lincoln keeping his gun aimed at a point a few feet above his head. Then, in confirmation of Lincoln's attuned senses, a footfall sounded and a form appeared on the edge of the circle of firelight.

'Hello to the camp,' a familiar voice said, although Lincoln couldn't place where he'd heard this man before. 'Can I join you?'

'Only if you put those hands where I can see them,' Lincoln said.

A man stepped into the firelight with his hands raised. He nodded to Daniel, who returned a smile before he turned back to Lincoln.

'I won't be taking on Samuel alone,' he said. 'My brother's coming with me.'

CHAPTER 4

'How long can you be away?' Daniel asked Henry when they'd ridden along for a few miles.

They were heading north-west, past Dougal's Ridge, aiming to meet up again with the river eighty miles south of their destination. Despite Lincoln's lack of interest in their mission, last night he had agreed to stay with them until they reached Skull Bend.

After that they would be on their own.

'I have leave for a week,' Henry said, 'but the military are interested in Samuel Holdstock too, so I may be able to stay away for longer, depending on what we find out.'

'It's a pity,' Lincoln said, 'that you couldn't bring reinforcements. You'll need them.'

Henry shrugged. 'Maybe next time.'

Lincoln shook his head. 'You go up against Samuel, there won't be a next time.'

'Then we're glad you came along to tell us how

we can stay alive,' Daniel said, unable to keep the sarcasm from his tone after repeatedly hearing Lincoln's downbeat assessment of their chances.

'Keeping myself alive is all I care about and you two should start thinking like that too.' Lincoln considered them, rubbing his chin. 'But maybe there is something I can do that'll help you survive for a few hours more than you'd manage on your own.'

Lincoln drew his horse to a halt and waited until the two men swung round to face him.

'We're listening,' Daniel said.

'In Empire Falls I learned that my quarry had gone to ground near Skull Bend in a two-bit excuse for a town called Indigo Ford. That was once a thriving settlement until Samuel came along.'

'That's an interesting tale,' Daniel said, 'but how will it help us?'

Lincoln sneered with a look that said he should have understood what he meant.

'Because men who hate Samuel gather there, and they're the only allies you'll get.'

Over the next two days Lincoln's two unwelcome partners said little as they rode along.

They always kept within a few miles of the river, which gradually became foam-flecked and moiling, showing why many still called it the Savage River. For most of the year it was a placid, easily fordable expanse, but for a few months every year it deserved its reputation as a river whose power should be

34

admired but avoided.

Around noon, they approached the river after a detour around a ridge, coming out at a wide sweeping bend. Lincoln drew to a halt on a rise and pointed out a sprawling collection of buildings nestling beside the water.

'Skull Bend,' he said.

'From a mile away,' Daniel said, 'it looks no different from Empire Falls.'

'It doesn't, but if you've got any sense, this is the closest you'll get.'

'Then I guess,' Henry said, 'we can't have any sense.'

Lincoln blew out his cheeks in exasperation. Then he directed them to swing their horses away back downriver.

Later, several shacks came into view at a point where the river widened to provide a shallow crossing point during the summer months.

Most of the buildings were derelict; some had been burnt down. One building though had several horses outside, and Lincoln moved on towards it.

Only when they'd dismounted did he turn to Daniel and Henry.

'Don't hinder me,' he said, 'and I'll show you someone who can help you.'

With that statement of intent, he headed inside into what had once been a thriving saloon. The two men trailed behind.

It'd been some time since he'd last been here

and, as he'd expected, the place was even more run down than the last time. Three men were whiling away the afternoon sharing a jug of ale around a table. Two of them were chatting while the third man had his head bowed.

Lincoln firmed his jaw, forcing himself to stay calm. One of the customers was Marshal Cliff Stroud and, as he'd told Daniel, he couldn't bring Samuel Holdstock's right-hand man to justice just yet.

Another customer, Wilson Piper, was leaning on the rough-hewn slab of wood that served as a bar.

The barman appraised him with a narrow-eyed glare that acknowledged he'd recognized him, then flicked his gaze to Stroud's table with a practised warning.

'What do you want, Marshal?' he asked. He spoke louder than was necessary in case anyone had failed to spot that a lawman had arrived.

Stroud didn't look up while Daniel and Henry stayed by the door leaving Lincoln to pace slowly across the room to the bar.

'Adna Burroughs,' he said.

'Never heard of him,' the bartender said without even a moment's pause to consider.

Lincoln rubbed his jaw as if he were considering this information, the motion masking his glance at Wilson, who was looking straight ahead and studiously avoiding catching his eye.

'In that case I'll leave.'

Lincoln turned away and paced by Wilson, who moved his head a fraction to listen to Lincoln's progress. That reaction was enough for Lincoln. He slapped both hands on his shoulders, spun him round and threw him back against the bar.

Wilson grunted as he hit the wood. Then he moved to spring back and throw himself at Lincoln. But he was too slow. Lincoln stopped him with a raised hand to the chest. Then he gathered a firm grip of his collar and drew him up to stare into his eyes.

'Get off me,' Wilson muttered.

'Only when you talk.' Lincoln flared his eyes. 'Where's Adna Burroughs?'

'I don't know nothing about him.'

Wilson darted his gaze past Lincoln's shoulder, looking for help, but a glance around the saloon confirmed he wouldn't get it. Marshal Stroud was making a show of not watching this confrontation and the bartender had backed away into the shadows.

'Don't believe you. Nothing happens here that you don't know, and Adna came here. So speak or we'll go outside. Only one of us will return.'

Wilson glared defiantly at him. Lincoln returned his glare and backed it up by slamming him back against the bar again.

'Go away,' Wilson whimpered. 'I'd sooner die than help you.'

Despite the words, Wilson shot him an imploring

glance and then flicked his gaze to Stroud's table.

Lincoln nodded, getting Wilson's meaning that, as he was on public view, he wanted a way out of his predicament.

'If I remember it right, the first time we met I dunked you in the water trough outside the old barn.'

'It didn't bother me,' Wilson said with a smirk. 'I was due a bath.'

'The second time I threw you in the river from the pier.'

'I enjoyed the swim.'

'The last time I tied you to a stall in the stables and took pot shots at you.'

'You're all talk, Marshal,' Wilson murmured. 'Leave me alone.'

Lincoln caught his change in tone. With an angry grunt, he threw him aside. As Wilson straightened his clothing, Lincoln turned away. He cast a glare at Stroud that the corrupt marshal didn't return, and then headed to the door with heavy, deliberate paces.

On the way he picked up Daniel and Henry and they scurried along beside him as he walked to the stables.

'What are we doing now?' Daniel asked.

'We are doing nothing,' Lincoln said. 'I have the information I came here for. Now you can go and get yourself shot up in Skull Bend.'

'But you promised to take us to someone who

could help us.'

Lincoln stomped to a halt and considered both men.

'I did, but you'll have to make your own arrangements.' Lincoln pointed back to the saloon. 'The man you want is Wilson Piper.'

With a smile on his lips, Lincoln carried on alone to the stables, leaving his unwelcome companions standing in bemused shock. At the door he looked back.

Daniel and Henry were making their slow way to the saloon, shaking their heads and murmuring unhappily to each other. Lincoln snorted a laugh and then peered into the darkened interior.

Four horses were inside, one being saddled up. Along one side the hayloft overhung the stalls. From the door most of this loft space was out of view, but there were wide gaps in the timber flooring.

Lincoln paced to the side while keeping his back to the wall, to stand beneath the hayloft. Only the roof was visible through the gaps above his head. As there wasn't a ladder up to this space, he judged that the pile of hay in the far corner was the most likely place for Adna to be hiding.

He paced on beside the stalls, darting his gaze to the hay, the horses and the hayloft above. When he reached the heap of hay, he picked up a rusted pitchfork and hefted it. Then he thrust it down into the edge of the hay.

The rickety prongs twanged. Lincoln moved

forward and slammed the fork down again, this time a few feet into the heap. The rattle of the prongs reverberated around the stables.

Lincoln grunted to give Adna another warning, then thrust down again. A screech sounded from within the heap and in a shower of hay a man stood with his hands raised.

'Enough!' he shouted. 'I'm not getting holed.'

Lincoln considered the man's shadow-shrouded form and the straw that masked his features. He transferred the fork to his left hand so he could free his gun hand. Then he pointed with the pitchfork, signifying that the man should stand in a slash of light cast through a hole in the wall.

With a shake that freed more hay from his head and shoulders, the man slouched away for a few paces, then turned to face him.

Lincoln appraised him. Then he shook his head.

'You're not Adna Burroughs,' he said.

'I never said I was.' The man smirked as he flicked his gaze up with an unconscious movement.

Lincoln followed his gaze as a timber creaked above. A form emerged from the recesses of the hayloft and leapt down. Lincoln started to swing the fork up to meet the falling man, but he was too slow and the man slammed into his chest, throwing him on to his back.

Lincoln lay sprawled on the ground, stunned and defenceless. But his attacker was more concerned with escape. Rapid footfalls receded away. Then a horse whinnied and hoofbeats clopped.

Lincoln got to his knees and looked up to see the horse and rider hurry by. The rider glanced at him and tipped his hat, letting him see that he was in fact his quarry Adna. Then he reached the door and disappeared from view.

Lincoln got to his feet and cast an irritated glare at the other man.

'He saw you coming,' the man said while backing away. 'He didn't give me no choice.'

Lincoln dismissed his role in the escape with an aggrieved grunt and hurled the fork into the hay. He headed to the door.

When he peered outside Adna was galloping out of town, leaving behind only a cloud of dust.

'The lawman's gone,' Wilson Piper said, facing Daniel and Henry. 'So why are you still here?'

'Because we weren't with him,' Daniel said. 'We came to see you.'

Wilson looked them up and down with a gleam in his eye that showed he was more confident now that Lincoln had left town.

'I don't want to see you.' He pointed to the door and then turned his back on them.

'You haven't heard what we want.'

Daniel waited for Wilson to respond, but he merely stood at the bar looking ahead.

Henry grunted to himself and stood on Wilson's other side.

'We're after Samuel Holdstock,' he said.

His lack of subtlety made Daniel cast him an irritated glare, but that was as nothing compared to the shocked look Wilson shot him.

'Keep your mouth shut,' he muttered, his voice low. 'Men have died for saying less.'

'We'd heard this was a safe place beyond his influence.'

'You heard wrong.' Wilson raised his voice. 'We all like what he's done for Skull Bend. We just come here for the peace and quiet.'

The bartender cast Wilson an amused glance. Then he considered the men at the table before shaking his head, making Wilson breathe a sigh of relief.

'Enjoying the quiet,' Daniel said with a narrow-eyed glare at Henry that told him to let him speak from now on, 'is why we're here.'

Wilson appraised them. 'So you're interested in a horse, then?'

Daniel considered Wilson's fixed stare. He nodded.

'We'll see what you have to offer.'

Wilson beckoned them to follow him. Nobody said anything else until they were outside and in clear space where they couldn't be overheard.

'What do you want?' Wilson said, while dawdling along with a casual air that gave no hint to anyone who might be watching that they were discussing serious matters.

'Our father died this week,' Daniel said. 'Samuel was involved.'

Wilson accepted this version of events with a brief shrug.

'It happens. Can you prove it?'

Henry and Daniel looked at each other and frowned, acknowledging that speaking openly about their aims might be unwise when they'd yet to work out a plan. But Daniel reckoned that Henry had been right to take a risk earlier, so he stopped before the stable door, stood tall, and put on a confident tone.

'No, but we aim to kidnap Samuel and take him to Empire Falls. Once he's in a cell, we'll shake him until we can prove what he's done. Then he'll face trial and get the justice he deserves.'

Wilson registered his surprise with an openmouth stare, but when both men nodded, he tipped back his hat and whistled.

'And there was me thinking you were another couple of idiots with a ham-fisted plan to shoot him up.' He laughed and then slapped a raised knee. 'So, if that's your plan I guess I'll have to help you.'

'Obliged. Will anyone else help?'

Wilson winked and then motioned them to join him in heading into the stables. Inside, one man was shovelling hay, but when he sensed that they'd come in, he turned to face them and scowled.

'This is Nathan Dobie,' Wilson said. 'If you want

to take on Samuel, he's the most trustworthy man you could want to meet.'

CHAPTER 5

'This is as far as we go,' Wilson Piper said, drawing his horse to a halt on the top of the rise where, a few hours earlier, Lincoln had first showed them the town.

Ahead, the buildings of Skull Bend hugged the land like a straggling line of rats fleeing the water. A pall of smoke hung over the town, masking the prosperity that the town apparently enjoyed.

'Obliged you've brought us this far,' Daniel said. 'But what about the rest?'

Wilson rubbed his chin as he glanced at Nathan Dobie, his pensive look appearing to silently ask his opinion on how much they could trust them to deliver on their promises. Nathan gave a small nod, then turned to them.

'Samuel promised us,' Nathan said, 'that if he saw us in town again, he'd kill us.'

'You have to be careful,' Daniel said, 'but if there's anything more you can do to help, we'd appreciate it.'

'The best we can offer is: we'll wait here. If you can reach us, we know places where you can hide Samuel until you can make plans to get him to Empire Falls.'

'But only,' Wilson said, leaning forward, 'if you get here alone. If you come riding out of town a-shooting in all directions with his gunslingers on your tail, we'll let you ride on by.'

Daniel frowned, but Henry managed a smile.

'That's a fair offer,' he said. He looked into town. 'Where will we find him?'

'In the Steamboat Saloon.' Nathan winked. 'You should be able to find it.'

Daniel peered into town and then smiled. In the middle of town, an old steamboat had been moored beside the pier. The faint and distant sounds of revelry from within reached them on the late afternoon air.

'And he owns the saloon?'

'He owns the town, but that doesn't stop him worrying that someone might take a shot at him. So he rarely leaves the safety of the boat and he never leaves the protection of his gunslingers.'

Daniel and Henry exchanged glances, sighing as they acknowledged that with every piece of information they gathered, their reckless and ill-thought-out plan sounded less likely to succeed.

'Any advice on how we can get close to him?'

'Most people who get close to him end up dead,'

Nathan said.

Wilson smiled. 'He's right, but there's only two ways you'll meet him. Which one will work depends on how well you play poker.'

'Pa didn't like us playing,' Daniel said, 'but we know what to do.'

Nathan nodded. 'Winners interest Samuel. If a stranger comes into his saloon, takes on the gamblers, and wins a thousand dollars, he'll want to talk to them.'

'A thousand!' Daniel spluttered. He patted his pockets, rattling the nickels and dimes that were the sum total of their combined wealth.

'I guess from your expression that you've not played for those sorts of stakes before?'

'We sure haven't,' Daniel said. Henry backed up his comment with a bemused shake of the head.

Wilson shrugged. 'In that case, you'll have to try the second way.'

Lincoln was gaining on Adna Burroughs.

After fleeing the stables, Adna had headed away from the river. Then he'd tried several detours that had failed to throw Lincoln off his tail. Now he was heading downriver back to Indigo Ford.

Adna was repeatedly looking across the river, presumably looking for a place to cross. In the quick moving water, he would be unlikely to succeed, but if he were to reach the other side first, Lincoln would be vulnerable in the water, and so he gathered a burst of speed from his mount.

Adna looked over his shoulder and saw Lincoln bearing down on him. He scrambled for his rifle sheath, but then he swayed in the saddle and thought better of trying to shoot while riding along the banks of the river.

Lincoln drew up behind him and urged his straining mount to draw alongside. Adna risked another glance at him. Then, in a reckless move, he veered away to head down the bank towards the river.

In a cloud of dust, his horse went skittering away, but the slope proved to be too steep and after a few paces it stumbled. Adna went flying forward from the saddle.

Lincoln didn't follow him. Instead he rode on by, along the top of the bank. He expected Adna to suffer a bone-crushing fall, but his momentum let him tumble head over heels twice until, in an explosion of water, he rolled into the river.

At a controlled rate Lincoln drew his horse to a halt and then made his way down the bank. When he reached the edge of the water, Adna's horse was trotting away from him while Adna had stood up with the water lapping around his waist. He shook himself, caught sight of his horse, and then set off after it through the shallows, using a stumbling gait.

Lincoln cantered along in a calm manner and drew alongside his quarry before he'd managed to get out of the water.

'Time to give up,' Lincoln said.

Adna stomped to a halt in the shallows. He flexed his back while darting his gaze to either side, weighing up his chances.

His horse was thirty yards away and still trotting along the otherwise smooth bank, which wouldn't provide him with any suitable places to which he could head. He stomped his feet with a show of being obstinate.

'You want to arrest me,' Adna pointed at the water, 'come in and get me.'

'That's tough talking for an unarmed man.'

Adna raised his fists and stood sideways on to him.

'Your orders are to take me alive, and I'm tough enough to best you.'

Lincoln set his horse square on to the water and peered at Adna, shaking his head. Then he reached back and unfurled a length of rope. Adna tensed in readiness for the fight to come, but Lincoln didn't intend to indulge him.

He hefted the rope in his right hand and then played it out, letting Adna see that he'd already fashioned a noose. Then he swirled the rope twice over his head, the motion making Adna drop his fists and feint to the left and right.

Lincoln followed the rhythm of his movements and then hurled the lasso. At the last moment Adna flinched away and avoided it coming down over his head and shoulders, but the rope caught around his left arm.

He tried to shake the rope loose, but with a snap of the wrist Lincoln drew it taut around his forearm.

As Adna tore at the rope with his free hand, Lincoln drew him in. Hand over hand he dragged him to the edge of the water.

'Quit struggling and kneel down,' Lincoln said, pointing to a strip of dry land a few feet from the water.

Adna gave one last irritated tug on the rope. Then his shoulders slumped and he did as ordered.

'It's a long way to Ash Creek,' he said. 'You'll never get me there.'

Ash Creek was the scene of his last attempted bank robbery, a town that despite his failure to get away with any money would be sure to deal with him harshly after he'd wounded a teller.

'Ash Creek won't care what state you're in when I hand you over to justice.' Lincoln waited until Adna winced. Then he rolled from the saddle and stood before him. 'So be smart. Hold out both hands and I'll let you ride there. Do something stupid and I'll drag you there.'

Adna gulped and moved his hands together, seemingly in a show of resignation, although his surly gaze suggested he was planning deception.

Lincoln still paced up to him, playing out the rope so that he could loop it around both hands. He swung the rope, but when it reached its zenith, Adna acted.

He flicked his hands away from the rope, then jerked his right hand to the side, exposing the knife he'd secreted in the sleeve. With a firm snap of the wrist, the knife came to hand. He slipped it under the rope that bound his arm and sliced through it.

Lincoln threw his hand to his holster, but before he reached his gun Adna grabbed the trailing end of the rope with his freed hand and gave it a sharp tug, dragging Lincoln forward for a pace.

To avoid stumbling into Adna, Lincoln thrust out a leg, but his assailant had already gained the advantage he'd sought. He threw himself at Lincoln while sweeping the knife round in a savage arc that aimed to slice into Lincoln's chest.

Lincoln jerked away from the intended blow. The knife parted only air until it caught in a trailing end of his jacket and held.

Adna grunted in irritation and lunged forward, aiming to stick Lincoln despite the blade being tied up in the cloth. Adna's hand hit Lincoln below the bottom rib, making Lincoln wince in expectation of the pain to come. Then Lincoln found, to his delight, that the cloth had encased the knife and he'd merely been punched.

From close to Lincoln glared at Adna. Then he headbutted him. He aimed to flatten his nose, but at the last moment Adna saw the blow coming and he recoiled away. Even so, Lincoln's forehead still caught him a glancing blow to the cheek that rocked him backwards.

Adna steadied himself and then tried to tear the knife free. When he failed, Lincoln added to his problems by twisting out of his jacket, leaving a bundle of cloth wrapped around Adna's wrist.

With a grunt of anger, Adna gave up trying to free himself and leapt at Lincoln. His momentum bundled him on to his back and in short order Adna was pressing down on him, but since Adna had only one hand free Lincoln wasn't unduly worried.

With a contemptuous shove he tipped him to the side and they rolled towards the river.

After two rolls Lincoln dug in an elbow aiming to still their motion, but Adna was struggling so much that Lincoln couldn't stop them and they carried on. They rolled twice more, then the cold slap of water splashed against Lincoln's side.

They came to a halt in the shallows with Adna lying on his back and Lincoln bearing down and keeping Adna's knife hand trapped between their chests. Adna threw a weak punch at his face, but Lincoln caught his wrist and then grinned.

'Let me go,' Adna gasped, struggling, but achieving nothing more than to muddy the water.

Lincoln bunched a fist with his free hand and held it high.

'You're under arrest,' he said. 'The only question you have to answer is how many times you want me to punch you before you give in.'

'I said get—'

Lincoln jabbed his fist down, giving him a light

punch to the cheek that still slapped his head back into the water.

'I'm still waiting for an answer.'

Adna clamped his mouth tightly shut and put all his efforts into trying to buck Lincoln, but the lawman bore down with all his weight and Adna could do nothing but squirm.

Presently he stopped struggling. Lincoln gave another significant glance at his fist and raised his eyebrows. Adna opened his mouth to snap back a retort, but then his gaze darted to the side a moment before a man spoke up behind them.

'Now what do we have here?'

Lincoln flinched with annoyance that someone had arrived without him noticing. He looked over his shoulder to find that the men who had been in the saloon in Indigo Ford were peering at them.

Marshal Cliff Stroud had come down the bank while the other rider stayed at the top. A third man was on foot with his head lowered.

'This man's my prisoner,' Lincoln said, 'Marshal Stroud.'

'Nobody takes prisoners near my town,' Stroud said.

'I'm Marshal Lincoln Hawk. What goes on in Skull Bend is no concern of mine and what I do outside Skull Bend is no concern of yours.'

Stroud cast him a sceptical glance. 'You're no marshal.'

Lincoln held his prisoner down as he unfurled

the jacket from around Adna's wrist, but then he found that his badge was no longer there. He looked around to see where it had shaken loose, the motion letting him see that both riders had turned guns on him.

'My badge is here,' Lincoln said. 'Turn those guns on this one while I find it.'

'The guns are on both of you,' Stroud said, 'because you two are under arrest.'

CHAPTER 6

'Samuel Holdstock sure is doing well,' Henry said.

Daniel nodded as he considered the huge side-wheeler. With evening falling, bright lights lit up the main saloon room along with the pier on one side and the river on the other. The closer they got, the louder became the sounds of revelry coming from within.

The only gangway on to the main deck was in the centre of the boat and to the side of the paddle-wheel. The craft appeared as if it were ready to sail, but the thick ropes that tied it to the pier at both ends were matted and mildewed, confirming that it hadn't ventured out on to the open waters for some time.

Once though, Wilson had told them, the side-wheeler and its six boilers had ruled the Big Muddy until other boats with bigger boilers had come along and relegated it to the backwaters and then to disuse.

Two guards on either side of the gangway tipped their hats to the customers as they went on board, but the brief conversations Daniel overheard confirmed that they were regulars. When the guards saw who was planning to come on board next they eyed them with suspicion and moved in to block their way.

'Time for us to stop being Daniel and Henry,' Daniel said, 'two decent folk from Empire Falls.'

'I don't pretend,' Henry said, standing tall. Then he uttered a heavy sigh. 'But we've come this far. . . .'

Daniel nodded, then set his face into what he hoped was a winning smile.

'Am I right in thinking,' he called out when he was still ten feet away from the guards, 'that this is Samuel Holdstock's steamboat?'

The nearest guard set his hands on his hips while the other man pointed to the huge sign above the windows of the main room, which proclaimed: Samuel Holdstock's Steamboat Saloon.

Daniel stopped to tip back his hat and peer at the sign with a blank expression that implied he couldn't read.

'We've come to the right place,' Henry said, speaking with a loud tone that he probably employed when addressing his troopers. 'Come sunup we'll be even richer.'

'We sure will,' Daniel said, rubbing his hands with glee. 'And the way our luck is running, we'll own the place by sundown tomorrow.'

They both faced the guards and put on cheerful expressions. The guards glanced at each other and exchanged pained looks that said they'd met numerous fools like them before. And that the only thing they'd be doing to them before sun-up was throwing them down the landing stage after someone had fleeced them of every cent they owned.

'Then,' one guard said, 'the Steamboat Saloon is the right place for two gentlemen like you.'

They both stood aside and beckoned them on. Maintaining their disguise, Daniel and Henry chortled and slapped each other on the back as they paced on to the gangway. Then they continued to exchange boasting comments as the guards sniggered behind them.

On the hardwood main deck two more guards frisked them for weapons and took possession of their six-shooters, while offering threats as to what would happen if they caused trouble. Then the brothers moved on to the saloon room.

Double doors were set before steps that led down into the sunken floor of the main room, most of which was given over to gaming tables and around which a few customers sat. Attracting more interest were the poker games, of which a dozen were in progress.

Daniel and Henry stood to the side and took in the scene. It didn't take them long to identify the high-stakes game in progress.

Set in clear space and waited on by two attentive bartenders, one table had attracted four smartly dressed businessmen who were eyeing their cards through a haze of cigar smoke.

The pot almost filled the table, so, on the raised dais behind the table, several gun-toting men wearing red jackets that identified them as working for the saloon were watching with interest.

'Seen Samuel yet?' Henry asked.

'Nope.' They had a decent description of him, but if Wilson was right, he only showed outside his quarters when there was heavy gambling going on.

'Then we'd better start there,' Henry said, nodding to a table that had been pushed up against a wall and on which several men were playing a good-natured game for what looked like dimes.

'We can't play with the small-time players. We're supposed to be rich fools.'

'Men who are pretending to be rich fools still need money.' Henry waited until Daniel snorted a laugh. Then he pointed at the nearest gaming table. 'I'm good at faro. I'll try to build up a stake for a bigger table.'

Daniel frowned and considered the main table. A showdown was imminent as the gun-toters had edged forward, but, as it turned out, they weren't needed.

After laying down cards, a ripple of applause sounded. Then one man drew the pot to him and another man stood, shaking his head. He made his excuses and then headed to the bar with the stiff-backed posture of a man trying to appear unconcerned by his loss.

The remaining players gesticulated and talked animatedly about the hand, while showing no sign of starting a new hand quickly.

'Being careful is the sensible option,' Daniel said. 'But a place has just opened up at the main table.'

Henry stared at him in open-mouthed shock.

'I've only played poker with you once and you were a good bluffer, but you'll never bluff your way into that game.'

'We won't know until I try.' Daniel winked and then beckoned him to follow. 'Now, try to look rich and foolish.'

'I can manage one of those,' Henry grumbled, but he still followed.

They weaved through the tables to reach the edge of the clear space around the main table. Daniel nodded to Henry, indicating that he should stay here.

Then he stood tall and plastered the eager smile on his face that he'd used to get past the guards. With the gun-toters glaring at him from the dais, he crossed the open space to reach the table. None of the players acknowledged him as they continued to talk, but that didn't stop him from clamping a hand on the spare chair.

'I got a chair here at last,' he declared using a

loud and annoying tone. He looked around. 'You playing for enough to make it worth my while?'

The players broke off from their conversation to assess him. It was unlikely that his rough and trail-dirty clothing would impress them and, sure enough, the man who had just won pointed to the side-tables.

'You'll find it worth your while,' he said with a mocking pleasant tone, 'to join one of those games.'

Daniel glanced at the indicated tables. He shook his head.

'I used to play at those sorts of tables.' He licked his lips. 'But that was before I got lucky.'

The winner started to shake his head, but the man to his right leaned forward.

'How lucky?' he asked.

'I haven't got much cash.' Daniel pulled out the few bills Wilson and Nathan had lent him. He cast them a disgusted glare as if by touching them he was soiling his hands. 'But when I've cashed this in, I'll have plenty.'

Daniel drew a small bag from his pocket by its drawstring and deposited it on the table with a satisfying thud. Eyebrows were raised as the players considered it, along with the second bag which he withdrew from his other pocket and hefted on a palm.

'And what is this?'

'Gold dust,' Daniel said. He delivered a resounding whoop. 'We've been prospecting.'

'There's no gold around here.'

'That's what everyone said, but we heard about the worked-out mine at Copper Town.'

'The gold there ran out years ago.'

Daniel winked and slipped on to the chair. He drew it forward to the table while beckoning everyone to join him in a conspiratorial huddle. When he had everyone's attention, he slipped the bags of dirt back into his pockets before anyone showed too much interest in them.

'Except we found an old map and spotted something nobody else had.' Daniel eyed everyone around the table, grinning. 'We backed our hunch, got lucky, and now I'm looking to continue the streak.'

He settled back in his chair, sporting an eager grin.

The players cast glances at each other of the kind that the guards had directed at them, conveying that they were wondering how big a fool he might be. The answer came when the winner picked up the deck of cards.

'Then,' he said, 'we'd better find out how much longer your lucky streak can last.'

Thirty minutes later, Daniel was $200 up. Then again, he'd expected that.

The winner of the hand before he'd joined, Edward Milton, had staked him fifty dollars so that he could start. Then Daniel went on to win the first hand on the strength of a displayed ace without

61

even having to turn over his hole cards.

It was only twenty dollars, but he made the most of his success by whooping and punching the air. Two hands later, he'd repaid the money he'd been loaned. Then he had embarked on building a pile of bills.

Soon his luck would change when the other players deemed he'd been lulled into being reckless. But he played along with the charade and grinned as Edward took his turn to deal out the cards for the next hand.

This time he dealt Daniel two face-up eights and a six and although his face-down hole card of a five didn't help him, two players folded before the final, face-down river card. Edward stayed in with two exposed sevens and a king.

This was the first time the game had progressed this far and so, putting aside the reason for his having come here, Daniel considered his options properly. He presumed that, as Edward could see he had the superior exposed hand, he was either trying a brazen bluff to test him out or he had another seven or king.

He decided he would be foolish to back out without paying to receive the river card. When Edward dealt this card and Daniel raised a corner to see he'd been dealt another eight, he had to suppress a smile.

With three eights, his hand would almost certainly beat Edward's. He raised fifty dollars, which

Edward matched and so, for the first time in his life, he locked horns in a high stakes poker game.

Within a minute his winnings were in the pot and Edward had raised him again. He had to either fold or bet on. He bit his bottom lip, trying to appear nervous, then withdrew a bag from his pocket.

'I haven't had this weighed,' he said, letting his voice shake for the first time, 'but I reckon there's five hundred dollars' worth of dust. It'll cost you that to stay in the game.'

Without a moment's hesitation, Edward matched his bet with cash and raised again.

'It's the same for you,' he said and leaned back.

The other players chuckled, enjoying seeing the subterfuge of the last thirty minutes come to a head with this sudden and possibly disastrous change of fortune.

Daniel considered the cards, judging that even if he were playing with his own money, albeit for a fraction of the stakes, he would bet on. So, after glancing at Henry, who was standing stiff-backed and pensive as he watched proceedings, he withdrew the second bag from his pocket, tossed it on the pot, and called.

Edward kept his expression impassive as he turned over his hole card, displaying the king Daniel had expected. Daniel was reaching out to flip over his river card to present his better hand when Edward turned over his own river card.

It was the seven of diamonds.

'Full house,' he said, 'sevens over kings. So have you got both eights?'

The twinkle in his eye said he already knew the answer to that question.

'Just one,' Daniel murmured, pushing his cards away.

'You got any more of that lucky gold dust, or will you have to go back to Copper Town and get some more?'

The players laughed. Daniel kept a fixed smile until everyone had become silent.

'I won't have to go that far,' he said using his normal voice, 'to get more of what's in those bags. If you wait for five minutes, I'll be back with another ten.'

Two players chortled and pointed to the door, urging him to get them, but Edward cast him a narrow-eyed glare that said he'd understood his meaning. He poked one of the bags with suspicion and watched it fall over, his raised eyebrows showed that he'd noted the lugubrious way it settled.

He clicked his fingers, encouraging two guards to jump down from the dais and hurry over to the table. Using two disdainful fingers, he deposited the bag on the palm of the nearest man.

'Pour it on the table,' he said.

While Edward kept his gaze on Daniel, the man did as ordered. Sharp intakes of breath sounded as the pile of dirt grew. Edward cast it the merest flicker of a glance and then resumed glaring at him.

'What's this?' the guard asked.

Edward took a deep breath. 'This man staked himself into the game with a pile of dirt. I want what's owed to me.'

The guards cast amused glances at the other players, noting that this demand wouldn't be satisfied. Then one guard slapped a hand on Daniel's shoulder and dragged him to his feet while the other guard collected Henry.

'These men have nothing,' one player said.

'Perhaps,' Edward said with an exaggerated hurt tone that implied he would be using this incident later to exert pressure on the saloon management. 'So I want the Steamboat special.'

The guards nodded. Then Daniel and Henry were roughly dragged away from the table and to the dais.

'That means,' Daniel's captor said, 'you're seeing Samuel Holdstock.'

Henry and Daniel shot glances at each other that confirmed they were ready to look out for opportunities now that their plan was coming to its critical, and most dangerous, part.

Then they resorted to slouching and digging their heels in, forcing their escort to shove them along as they played their parts of being two chancers who had been caught out.

They were led across the dais while hoots of derision and mocking encouragement sounded from many of the customers.

At the back of the dais was a door that led them up a narrow flight of stairs to a corridor with a single door at the end. Silence greeted the sharp knock, so, after waiting for thirty seconds, the second man knocked more forcefully.

A grunt of irritation sounded within, followed by sounds of rummaging before the occupant spoke up.

'I heard you the first time. Go away.'

'There's two men here you need to see.'

'I doubt that.' A heavy sigh sounded. 'Show them in.'

They were dragged inside and deposited before a desk that faced the door. Samuel Holdstock, a rangy man, sat behind it running a finger down a column of figures cast within a large ledger.

His gaze was actually on a pile of bills that were trapped beneath an ornate letter-opener; apparently he was presenting the appearance of a busy man who had been interrupted.

When the silence had dragged on for long enough to be uncomfortable, he looked up and raised an eyebrow.

'They can't pay their debts,' one man said while pushing Daniel forward.

Samuel nodded. 'To the house?'

'It's not your money, but the problem is they played Edward Milton for a fool.' The guard snorted a laugh. 'They gambled using a bag of gold dust that turned out to be dirt.'

Samuel leaned back in his chair and laughed. The laughter continued until the guards joined in. Then he straightened his face in a moment.

'Edward being shown up as a fool is fine, but nobody must laugh at him. How angry is he?'

'He asked for the special.'

'Understandable, and with Stroud away I can't cut them loose.' Samuel turned his gaze on to Daniel and Henry for the first time. 'Do you have anything to offer to placate Edward?'

Anger clawed at Daniel's gut, making him want to tear himself away from the guards, leap at Samuel, and throttle him before he could be stopped. But he firmed his jaw to avoid showing his anger.

Their plan hinged on what happened next. But standing here, trapped deep within the lair of the man whom they aimed to bring to justice, brought home just how foolhardy that plan was.

The extent of their scheming had been to find a way to meet Samuel and then hope they could bundle him away off the boat to the waiting Wilson and Nathan. How they would do that Daniel had no idea, but as he struggled to find the right thing to say, Henry uttered a pained sigh and then began breathing deeply.

'We never meant Edward no harm,' he murmured, his voice cracking and sounding nothing like his usual assured tone. 'We can make this all right, but I can't breathe.'

Samuel glanced at the guard's hands, which were

on Henry's shoulders.

'Nobody is stopping you breathing . . . yet.'

'I can't breathe in small spaces.' Henry gasped and bent over. 'It's too close.'

Samuel gave him a critical look, then gave a slow nod.

'I've seen this condition before.' Samuel clicked his fingers and jerked a hand towards a door at the back of the room. 'We'll go up on deck where you can have all the air you need.'

Between frantic gasps Henry murmured his thanks. Then, with Samuel leading and the guards pushing them on from behind, they headed to the door.

They emerged in front of a short flight of steps that led up to another closed door. High windows were to one side, through which Daniel could see the night sky and, along with the growing coldness, this suggested that the steps led out on to the hurricane deck at the stern.

Henry continued to heave in racking gasps of air, but at the door he caught Daniel's eye. They couldn't exchange information, but their next actions were clear.

Samuel would go through the door first. Henry and Daniel would follow. Then there would be a moment when they were outside and the guards were on the steps. They would need to wrest themselves free, slam the door on the guards, and capture Samuel.

They would have only a moment, but they would have to use it to bundle him over the side and into the water. Having lived beside the river, they were strong swimmers, so once in the water, they would have the advantage and they stood a chance of reaching Wilson and Nathan.

So Daniel climbed faster to get ahead of Henry, giving him the task of shutting the door on the guards.

Samuel reached the door and pushed it open, receiving a blast of cold air. As the deck came into view, Daniel saw a white-painted rail ten feet ahead with nothing beyond, adding further hope that this was the stern beyond which there would be nothing below but water.

As it turned out, they had climbed higher than he thought and they were coming out on the top Texas desk, behind the pilothouse. Daniel relaxed, preparing to throw the guard's hands off him when he went through the door.

He sensed Henry tensing behind him as he prepared to carry out his part. Then he saw that Samuel wasn't alone. Several other men were on the steps down to the hurricane deck and they were turning to face them.

He counted seven men, and more were heading along the Texas deck to join them. He stopped and stood tall, as did Henry, as he accepted they would have to bide their time while they awaited another opening to bundle Samuel away.

The guards pushed them on towards the steps. The men who had been waiting for them parted, letting them move down the steps and on to the hurricane deck. At the rail they looked down.

To Daniel's irritation what they saw was the main deck, which circled the saloon room. Although they could jump down to the water from the stern, from this position they couldn't.

On the main deck people had come outside. Their arrival made many of them point up and chat animatedly amongst themselves.

Edward Milton was standing alone and glaring at the hurricane deck with his arms folded. Samuel gestured to him and this made him relax and join the others.

'What are we doing out here?' Henry said.

Samuel considered him. 'I'm pleased that your breathing has improved now that we're outside.'

With a smirk on his lips, he signified that one of his red-coated men should approach. This man drew a sword out from behind his back. He held it high in salute, and then laid it on Samuel's outstretched palms.

'I can breathe easier up here,' Henry said, taking a deep breath as, like Daniel, he eyed the sword with bemusement.

'You'll need your new-found strength.' Samuel swished the sword through the air. 'But I can see you're wondering why I have this magnificent weapon, so I'll put your mind at rest. This was a gift from my old friend Major Delany, the commanding officer at Fort Lord.'

'Stolen, more like,' Henry said, his surprise apparently making him forget that this revelation shouldn't shock a man who had been gold-prospecting at Copper Town.

'Maybe.' Samuel turned the blade to let a distant light shine first into Henry's eyes and then into Daniel's. 'But no matter what you believe, my contact in Empire Falls told me that after Marshal Ellis Moore's unfortunate demise, his two sons left town. The last that was heard of them, they were annoyed he'd been involved with—'

'Stop gloating!' Daniel snapped as a more intense dread clutched his stomach. 'What are you saying?'

Samuel lowered the sword to stick it point first into the deck. He leaned on the hilt.

'That I knew you and Henry were coming.' Samuel raised his eyebrows. 'That is who you are, isn't it?'

'Yes,' Daniel muttered through clenched teeth.

Samuel nodded to the guards, who spun them round, then pushed them up to the rail.

'In which case I'll take even greater delight in giving you the Steamboat special.'

CHAPTER 7

'Search the water,' Lincoln said. 'I'm a US marshal and my badge is here somewhere.'

While his deputy disarmed Lincoln, Marshal Stroud considered him and then his other two prisoners.

'I'm heading back to Skull Bend,' he said. 'I've not got the time to waste.'

'You have,' Lincoln muttered, his flaring eyes making Stroud back away for a pace. 'Unless you want to deal with me.'

Stroud peered upriver, as if he were considering the request, although when he turned back his smile showed he hadn't. Then he removed the smile and lowered his tone to an honest-sounding one.

'I deliver justice in Skull Bend, and I deal with everyone in the same way. That includes you.'

The prisoner whom Stroud had taken earlier muttered to himself, suggesting that he didn't reckon that justice would turn out well for him.

Lincoln considered how he would deal with the situation, if their roles were reversed. As Stroud had arrested Adna too, when he'd expected he would release him, he gave a reluctant nod.

Stroud smirked, then gestured for everyone to move out. He and his deputy rode while they made the three men walk between them.

For an hour they moved on beside the riverbank, but despite Stroud's claim that he needed to reach town urgently, when the sun lowered towards the distant mountains, he called a rest.

Stroud and his deputy stood back and considered the prisoners with suspicion while they debated their arrangements for the night. On the journey, Lincoln had found out that the other prisoner was Clark Varley, although he hadn't found out what his crime had been. When Lincoln looked at him, Clark spoke for the first time.

'So,' he said, 'are you really a lawman?'

'Sure,' Lincoln said. He glanced at Adna for confirmation, but he clamped his mouth tightly shut.

'And why were you after him?' He nodded at Adna.

'He's a known associate of Samuel Holdstock and he's wanted for three failed bank raids in the last month. I was bringing him in before he got lucky.'

'Lucky!' Adna muttered to himself.

Clark smiled thinly. 'Luck's deserted us all, including you, lawman. You'll die, too.'

Adna buried his head in his hands, as if this

confirmed his worst fears, while Lincoln shook his head.

'Marshal Stroud isn't a dutiful lawman, but he won't kill a US marshal.'

'He will. Because that's what Samuel would want him to do.'

'Maybe, but he won't succeed and neither will he kill you.'

Clark shook his head in disbelief.

'Two nights ago, I lost money I didn't have at Samuel's gaming tables. It was either get killed or run. I ran, but I didn't get far. Now I'll die, but I'll have a lawman at my side.'

Adna uttered a pained bleat and looked up.

'That's my story too,' he whined.

'It's not,' Lincoln snapped. 'You tried to raid—'

'I didn't want to,' Adna babbled. He paused to bunch his hands, stilling a tremor. 'I didn't mean to shoot up that teller in Ash Creek and I was never an associate of Samuel. I just owed him money, but he caught me before I could run. He gave me a month to raise the money, and the only way I could do that was to steal.'

Lincoln shrugged. 'Then you were as bad at stealing as you were at gambling.'

Adna gave a rueful snort and lowered his head, leaving Clark to utter a sympathetic sigh.

'Nobody makes money off Samuel's gaming tables, but those tables make a lot of dead men.'

After that comment everyone resorted to silence.

Lincoln wasn't sure whether he should believe these tales, but he then ignored the prisoners while he looked out for an opportunity either to escape or take on Stroud.

When the sun set Stroud lit a fire and the two men carefully watched their prisoners.

Despite the late hour nobody ate and the lawmen showed no signs that they would feed them. Lincoln was wondering if this oversight might give him a reason to provoke an argument, and perhaps engineer a distraction, when he saw two riders coming downriver.

They dismounted and joined the lawmen. After a brief conversation, Stroud came over to stand before them.

'It's time to talk,' Lincoln said, standing to face the four men.

'It's not,' Stroud said with relish. 'It's time to release you.'

'Obliged,' Lincoln said cautiously.

'Don't be. Once you're free, I'll deem you to have escaped. Do you know how I deal with escaped prisoners?'

Lincoln narrowed his eyes. 'I'd guess you do whatever Samuel Holdstock tells you to do.'

Stroud glanced at the other men, who grinned eagerly.

'Sure. So you'll all be found with bullets in the back, like the others who owe Samuel. But I'm a reasonable man, so you get a choice.' Stroud laughed, the sound making the other men chuckle. 'You can either get shot in the back here, or you can give us some sport and run. I hope you'll run.'

Samuel Holdstock stood at the rail and breathed in deeply, making a show of enjoying the night air.

'What's the Steamboat special?' Daniel asked, despair tightening his stomach.

'Gamblers who run up debts with the house are usually run out of town,' Samuel said. 'Then they provide sport for men who enjoy hunting resourceful prey. But for those who can't repay their debts to other gamblers, an example that everyone can see is more appropriate.'

Daniel kept his mouth clamped tightly shut, refusing to give Samuel the satisfaction of a retort, but when the man holding Henry shoved him forward, he couldn't avoid asking the obvious question.

'What example?'

'My boat's been moored here for years, but it's still operational.' Samuel looked at the paddlewheel on this side of the boat. 'These days the wheels are used for a more interesting purpose.'

Daniel looked at the wheel and saw, after a few moments, in the shadow beneath the paddlebox, two bodies strapped to the wheel: Nathan Dobie and Wilson Piper.

'Dead?' Daniel murmured.

'Yes, but they were lucky. They were dead before

they were strung up.' Samuel smirked. 'You were followed from Indigo Ford, as was the lawman.'

As the shocking realization of what Samuel intended registered, one of the guards grabbed Henry and dragged him on towards the wheel.

Two guards joined them. In short order they tied him to a blade on the paddlewheel, placing him beneath the paddlebox and above the limp bodies of the two men who had made the mistake of helping them.

Henry didn't struggle. After all, with three men holding him, preserving his strength was more sensible. Further along the hurricane deck, two men held Daniel while a third stood beside Samuel.

The men holding Daniel talked in low tones as they awaited the entertainment. When the guards had finished their work, they left Henry and clambered down the wheel to stand on the main deck. Samuel raised his arms to draw attention to him.

'The Steamboat Saloon,' he announced, 'is the safest gambling haunt in the state. Tonight, I issue another warning to anyone who thinks they can abuse our hospitality.'

A cheer sounded while Edward Milton nodded with approval and swung round to watch the wheel.

From within the pilothouse on the Texas deck, a creak sounded as a lever was thrown. Then the wheel shuddered into motion, as did the wheel on the other side of the boat.

As the boat rocked, straining against the mooring

ropes, Henry looked along the hurricane deck, but the two men had secured Daniel and he could do nothing other than watch the wheel turn. It revolved away from him making Henry disappear from view under the paddlebox.

A minute later he emerged briefly, lying sideways on the blade. Then he moved out of view beneath the main deck.

The speed of revolution was slow and, with around a quarter of the wheel being under water, Daniel counted to forty before the damp ends of the already dunked blades reappeared.

Worse, they were clogged up with the debris from the river bottom.

With mounting trepidation, Daniel strained his neck, looking out for the first sign of his brother. When he appeared, he was coughing and struggling against his bonds, rotted vegetation and mud sloughing from his body.

Hoots of derision sounded from the watching people on the main deck and the catcalling continued until he disappeared from view again.

Samuel sidled along the deck to stand beside Daniel.

'Are you looking forward to your turn?' He waited for an answer that Daniel wasn't prepared to give. 'Don't worry. Henry might get lucky. It depends on where the wheel stops when I have you strapped to it.'

Samuel grinned as he eyed Daniel's discomfort.

'You sound as if you want something from me,' Daniel said, unable to mask the distress in his tone.

'I do, but I won't get it. You and Henry have an arrogant look that says you'd sooner die than beg for your life ... unlike your father. He gave up without a fight.' Samuel snorted a laugh when Daniel muttered an oath. 'But maybe there's an alternative.'

Samuel gestured up to the pilothouse and, with a grinding of gears, the wheel slowed its movement.

This time Daniel counted to fifty before Henry spun back into view, coughing and shaking his head to clear the mud from his face, after which gears ground again and the wheel slowed once more.

'You can't torture a man for entertainment,' Daniel muttered.

'I can because it shows I care about my customers.' Samuel moved round to stand beside him. He whispered in his ear. 'And when I've taken their money, I'll own them, like I owned your father, weak fool that he was.'

Daniel stiffened, refusing to be riled. 'I know the story of his downfall. The only mistake he made was meeting you,' he said through gritted teeth. 'I'll make sure he's the last one to suffer.'

'How?'

The men holding his arms tightened their grip, sensing he might act. Daniel glanced to either side, confirming that these three men were the only ones on the hurricane deck, but they were all armed and

79

watching him carefully.

'We'll prevail, and later we'll deal with you.'

'As a gambling man I can assure you that the odds are stacked against that happening.'

'A man who gambles with a rigged hand isn't a gambling man.'

Samuel's eyes flared before he blinked away the momentary irritation.

'I enjoy a genuine gamble.' He glanced at the wheel, noting that Henry was disappearing from view for another dunking. 'So I'll offer you one: fail and you both die now, win and you both die, but later, at a time of my choosing.'

'I accept.'

Samuel laughed. Then he gestured for his men to follow him. They led Daniel up the steps to the Texas deck and then to the pilothouse where Samuel entered first.

He issued brief orders, which led to the pilot leaving and only one of the guards taking Daniel inside.

The room was small, leaving space only for the three men to crowd around the row of pulleys, the two levers and the pilotwheel.

Daniel could only guess what the controls did, but Samuel drew his attention to the lever that the pilot had been operating. It came up to his shoulder and it was set into the floor at an almost perpendicular angle.

'To save communicating with the engineers, I had

this control lever for the paddlewheels added,' Samuel said, tapping it. 'Usually I slow them to give the man strapped to the wheel a longer dunking until he stops caring how long he stays under water.'

Samuel chuckled as he sat on the lazy bench that ran along the back of the pilothouse.

'And what's the gamble?'

Samuel beckoned the guard to push Daniel towards the lever.

'You'll stop the paddlewheel.' He made a pushing motion, showing Daniel how he should move it. 'If you stop it while Henry is in the water, you'll kill him. If he's out of the water. . . .'

Samuel smirked and left their subsequent fate unsaid, but Daniel ignored him. He thought back to how fast the wheel had been turning and where Henry had been when he'd last seen him. He judged there had been enough time for one revolution and that Henry would now be under water.

'Release me,' he said, 'and I'll take your gamble.'

CHAPTER 8

After a nod from Samuel, Daniel's guard released him and stood to the back of the pilothouse.

With a roll of his shoulders to free the cramps from his muscles, Daniel grabbed the lever and stared straight ahead. He mouthed numbers counting out Henry's imagined progress through the water.

The darkness beyond the pilothouse window let him see the guard's and Samuel's reflections, their faces dim in the light from the solitary oil lamp dangling from the roof.

'Round and round the wheel goes,' Samuel said, grinning as he swung his sword in a small circle, 'but where will it stop?'

Daniel judged that Henry would now be at the top of the wheel beneath the paddlebox, but he merely gathered a firmer grip of the lever as he waited for Samuel to become irritated.

'Forgive me, brother,' he whispered, 'for what

I'm about to do.'

Samuel stood up in anticipation, making the guard edge forward too. Still Daniel didn't act as he continued to count and imagine Henry now dropping below the main deck and then slipping under the water.

'Do it,' Samuel urged.

On the main deck, a sudden commotion followed by chortling cut through the general hubbub. The utterances were loud enough for Samuel and the guard to cast a look through the side window even though they wouldn't be able to see what was interesting the crowd.

That was the distraction Daniel had been waiting for.

'I choose now!' he shouted. He dropped backwards, dragging the lever with him and using the opposite action to the one required to stop the wheel.

With a ratcheted series of thuds, the lever swung down to a forty-five-degree angle, where it ground to a halt. Below deck, gears squealed and cogs protested as the wheels built up speed. A metallic crack sounded, suggesting his sudden motion had broken something and locked the lever in place.

The sudden motion had the desired effect and made the boat lurch and then strain against its mooring ropes. Daniel didn't like to think of the effect it would have on Henry as he went hurtling round on the wheel, but he put that worry from his mind and spun round.

The guard was dragging Samuel to the door as he acted to save Samuel rather than take Daniel on directly. Daniel leapt at them, aiming to wrest the gun from the guard's grasp. But the man swung Samuel through the door and then slammed the door shut behind him, causing Daniel to run into the door.

Daniel pressed his back to the wood, considering the empty pilothouse and wondering how he could use his potentially brief period of freedom to best effect. A gunshot tore through the front window, shattering glass. On the deck, Samuel's men were coming into view, so Daniel dropped to one knee.

He peered around. A shining object caught his attention and made him smile. In his haste to get outside, Samuel had dropped his sword.

Daniel hefted it, enjoying the feel of a weapon, but then gunfire splayed through the window. He pressed his back to the wall beneath the window as lead clattered around the small room. More glass shattered before the shooting stopped.

'He could still be alive,' Samuel shouted. 'Keep firing.'

Footfalls sounded on the timber decking as his men moved to come up to the window, where they'd be sure to see him kneeling down. That thought made him look up to the oil lamp swinging from the roof.

He rehearsed the motion in his mind before he

leapt up and swung the sword at the lamp. He caught it and sent it flying away to crash into the wall and then clatter to the floor, extinguishing the light. He carried on the motion to roll into hiding beside the wheel in the darkness.

A grunt of irritation sounded outside, then another burst of gunfire tore into the room, smashing the remaining windows. Then Samuel demanded that someone kick open the door.

Daniel didn't fancy his chances of defending himself with the sword. So he crawled along the floor, away from the door, then stuck the sword through the side window.

He rattled it from side to side to scrape away the shards of glass on the sill. Then he leapt to his feet and folded himself over the windowsill.

He just had enough time to note that none of the guards was on this side of the pilothouse. Then he tumbled on to the deck. He broke his fall with an outstretched arm and rolled to the side, where he pressed himself to the wall and took stock of the situation.

The door burst open, suggesting that nobody had seen his escape. So he sought to delay the moment of his discovery by sidling along the Texas deck and away from Samuel and the guards.

The deck circled round the pilothouse and several other darkened cabins. Daniel hurried on to the first cabin and tried the door. It was locked, as was the second. He continued on to the corner where he glanced back. To his delight nobody was in sight.

He slipped around the corner and put his shoulder to another door, but again it was locked. From the other side of the Texas deck, cries of alarm went up, presumably as the guards finished searching the empty pilothouse.

Keeping in the shadows, Daniel hurried to the rail at the back of the deck. Below was an unoccupied section of the hurricane deck.

He leaned over the rail and saw windows below that looked into the top of the saloon room. To his right was Henry's wheel now surging round and making the boat rock. To his left the other wheel was in deeper water and moving more freely.

He gulped, wondering how Henry would be faring, while the screams and sounds of consternation emanating from the main deck showed that his action had had the desired effect of creating chaos. He rolled over the rail, lowered himself down the wall, and jumped.

He made his way to a point above the entrance to the saloon room where he surveyed the scene. A stream of panicked and shouting people was running down the landing stage.

This chaos was even greater than he'd hoped to create and he soon saw the reason. The boat was straining the mooring ropes to their utmost.

At both ends of the boat the ropes were stretched taut, showing that the wheels weren't supposed to be turned at full speed while the boat was docked.

Then Daniel saw Henry go spinning round on the wheel. He was struggling and, when the wheel reached a point that was level with him, he raised himself to a sitting position and tore at his bonds before flopping down and disappearing from view.

Heartened, Daniel hurried on to the wheel, the sword held aloft as he planned how he could use it to cut Henry free.

Gunfire sounded, kicking splinters from the deck in front of his feet. He looked up to see that the guards were at the rail on the Texas deck above him.

As one they all sighted him. Daniel jerked one way and then the other, searching for the best place to hide, but he was in open space and light from the saloon windows was illuminating out his form in sharp relief.

With no other option, Daniel threw back his arm, ready to hurl the sword at the guards, but before he could release it a sharp crack resounded and the deck beneath his feet slid away, knocking him over. On his back he looked up, expecting to see lightning from a gathering storm that he hadn't been aware of, but the night sky was starry.

The noise continued, sounding like a thousand whips being cracked. Jerks of the deck accompanied each agonizing creak. He fought to sit up and saw that one of the guards was draped over the side and another man was dangling from the rail. The others weren't in sight.

He shook himself and got to his feet, swaying as he struggled to keep his footing. Sounds of screaming on the pier drew his attention and he was able to see what had happened.

The gangway was dangling free and no longer resting on the pier. A few people were hanging on to it; others were falling into the water.

Then the pier glided away from him until, in a sudden change of perspective, he saw that he'd been wrong. It was the boat that was gliding away from the pier.

The fast-turning wheels had put too much strain on the ropes that were holding the boat in place. The ropes at the stern had snapped and now the boat was swinging out into the water.

Daniel looked at the wheel, wondering how he could free Henry, but then he forced that matter from his mind and embarked on a tactic to sow more confusion.

He ran for the bow. Encountering no obstructions, he reached the rail above the boiler deck. He lowered himself down to that deck and then to the main deck. In short order he hurried over to the mooring ropes, these being the only ones that were stopping the boat from surging out into the water.

By the time he stood over the ropes the boat had swung out and was now pointing away from the pier; the turning wheels on either side were trying to pull it further away. The heavy ropes that stopped it moving were thicker than Daniel's arms and he couldn't move them unaided, but he had the sword and the tension had strained his muscles rigid.

Daniel raised the sword and swung it down on a cord. The sword bounced off with a dull clang, making Daniel feel as if he'd hit iron.

When his arms stopped shaking, he flexed his biceps and tried again, with the same effect, and then again. After ten slices, with each one getting increasingly weak as his strength gave out, he stood back.

While he rubbed his arms, he looked at the hurricane deck. Samuel's men were no longer visible, but he assumed they would be coming for him within moments.

He bent to consider the rope. To his relief he saw that his efforts had had an effect, after all. It was a small one, on only one split length of twine, but the sight heartened him. When he resumed swiping at the rope he concentrated on hitting this spot accurately rather than hitting with all his might.

Two more swipes split another length of twine, Then, without any further effort, others cords peeled away. He encouraged them with short swipes and, like bread being broken in two, the rope parted.

He turned and hurried away to avoid the whiplash as the broken rope snaked away into the water. Luckily, it didn't snap with the force Daniel had expected, as the remaining two ropes then took up the strain.

Daniel began work on the next one, using the technique that had worked on the first rope: using short swipes on one area.

Again, the first few blows had almost no effect, but as soon as he'd split the first length of twine, the rest were easier to fray. This time the rope started parting after he'd cut only three twines and he dived to the deck as the rope snapped with a heavy crack and slewed away.

He put the sword to the last rope, swiping quickly before he was discovered. He'd managed six blows and the first twirls of broken twine were sticking up when a harsh voice sounded behind him.

'Stop! This is over.'

He turned to find that Samuel had now caught up with him and that two gunmen were flanking him.

'The Steamboat surprise was more surprising than usual,' Daniel said. He snorted a laugh. 'Your customers will never forget this night.'

'They will, like they'll forget you. Now lower the sword.'

Daniel rolled his shoulders and glanced at the rope, seeing the cords stretched taut with several lengths of twine fraying and then snapping. He gave a resigned shrug.

'If you insist,' he said.

Then, with all his strength, he hammered the sword down on the breaking twine.

'Shoot him,' Samuel shouted, but the sword had

already bitten into the rope.

With a crack like thunder the rope parted, tearing the sword from Daniel's hand and sending him reeling. Then the boat broke loose and, with the wheels pounding out their insistent rhythm, it surged off into open water.

CHAPTER 9

'Keep going,' Lincoln muttered, pushing Clark onwards.

'I don't need to do nothing anyone says no more,' Clark whined as he stomped to a halt. 'I'm a free man.'

Adna uttered a harsh laugh and also pushed him along.

'You are,' he said, 'but not for long if you don't move.'

'Listen to Adna,' Lincoln said as Clark continued to grumble. 'He speaks sense.'

Clark shrugged, but then with an irritated grunt he moved on. At a steady trot, they carried on down the slope, heading away from the river.

Lincoln hadn't lied. He now accepted that his fellow prisoners Adna and Clark had been correct. Marshal Cliff Stroud not only worked for Samuel Holdstock; he rounded up anyone who owed his boss money, and then he used them for sport.

Accordingly, Stroud had given the three men ten minutes' start on foot before he came for them. Despite the dark, this wasn't a generous lead as the almost full moon had risen and through low scudding cloud it threw out their long shadows on the hard ground.

Lincoln reckoned their only hope was to find somewhere to hole up, but so far he hadn't seen any cover. So they'd had no choice but to run on, tracking west, hoping they'd get lucky. And by now Stroud would be in pursuit.

The slope they were heading down petered out on to flat plains. Low scrub created a grey sea that provided no cover. Only the occasional boulder emerged to provide some hope of their being able to hide in the dark shadows. But even in the low light their trampling passage through the scrub created an easy trail to follow, and their pursuers had claimed to be experienced manhunters.

That thought made Lincoln look around as he ran. He was an experienced manhunter too; maybe he could use the tactics that others had employed against him to avoid the hunters. But he didn't have long to act as the distant clop of hoofs was sounding at the top of the slope along with whoops as the pursuers enjoyed their hunt.

Adna glanced at him. 'Hear that?'

'Yeah,' Lincoln said, slowing to a halt. 'They'll be on us in a moment.'

While Clark hurried on, Adna stomped to a halt

and swung round to look back at the way they'd come with his hands set on his hips.

'We should make a stand here and hope one of us can wrest a gun off them.'

'You're right, except I'll get the gun.'

Adna frowned, but he joined Lincoln in watching Clark run on into the scrub, beating a path anyone could follow. Then, with a dart of his head, Clark looked to either side as he realized he was running alone.

He gestured at them. 'Move. They're coming.'

'We can't outrun them,' Adna said. 'But we have a plan.'

Clark glared at them, then looked up the slope. He waved a dismissive hand and turned away.

'I'll take my own chances,' he shouted as he ran on.

'Do that,' Lincoln said, speaking so that only Adna could hear, 'and you might help us.'

Two minutes later the riders came thundering down the slope. They followed the obvious trail through the scrub towards the distant fleeing figure which, in the moonlight, could easily be mistaken for a line of men.

Lying on his side in the low scrub, Lincoln watched them approach. From a distance his cover was adequate, but when the riders were closer, he and Adna, lying twenty yards away on the other side of the trampled scrub, would be easily visible. They must hope that the riders' attention would be on Clark.

Lincoln kept still as he watched Stroud lead the other three riders. Now that they were on level ground they had slowed to a steady trot, but they had formed a straggling line.

This was fine with Lincoln. He drew up his legs and put his weight on his right foot with his hands pressed to the ground.

Stroud went by, straining forward to peer into the gloom at Clark's distant figure. A few seconds later the second rider trotted by. He was leaning to the side as he peered past Stroud.

As the third man approached, Lincoln drew himself up, risking being seen, but the rider didn't look at him. The moment he passed, Lincoln leapt to his feet and hurried on to the trampled stretch of scrub to face the final rider.

Adna timed his appearance well as he hurried into view from the other direction.

Both men waved their arms, making their forms large. They jumped up and down in front of the rider as he bore down on them.

Standing before the speeding horse, Lincoln gritted his teeth, hoping that their sudden appearance would spook either the steed or the rider. For several long strides the steed galloped on, but then it balked at the sight of them standing in the way. It tried to veer away.

The rider fought to keep his mount on track as, for several heart-thudding moments, Lincoln and Adna faced the horse, unsure whether they should stay put or leap to the side. But as the horse loomed over them, it jerked away to the side, rearing with the sudden change of direction.

Self-preservation defeated bravery and both Lincoln and Adna rolled away in the other direction. They came to rest on their knees looking up at the rider, who was trying to calm his bucking horse as it rampaged around in a circle.

They added to his woes by running at him, shouting and kicking at the ground to raise dust while waving their arms.

A cry rent the air and the rider went tumbling from the saddle to crash to the ground on his back in an explosion of dust.

'Don't move,' Lincoln shouted to Adna. 'I'll deal with him.'

He didn't check that Adna had carried out his order, but hurried to the fallen man. He grabbed his vest front and yanked him to his feet, receiving only a groggy and feeble attempt to push him away. Then he thudded a short-armed jab to the man's cheek, which cracked his head back while releasing his grip so that he toppled over.

While the man lay sprawling, Lincoln slapped a hand on his holster, but to his irritation it was empty. He ran his hands over the man's jacket as he searched for a weapon, but to no avail. It must have shaken loose, he concluded.

He searched through the scrub without much hope, then looked up to seek out the horse, but to his surprise a dark shape loomed over him. Adna had ignored his order and he'd arrived, mounted up and smiling at his success in capturing the horse.

'Come on,' he said, holding out a hand. 'They haven't noticed us yet.'

Lincoln bit back his irritation and got to his feet. He cast a last look around for the sheen of gun-metal, but having failed to spot the lost gun he let Adna drag him up to ride doubled-up.

After confirming that they hadn't been seen, they set off at a canter back along the trail through the scrub. When they reached the slope and rockier ground, they veered back towards the river.

'This horse won't get both of us away,' Lincoln said.

'I know, but we're alive and that means we can think up another plan.'

Lincoln peered sideways into the gloom, but he couldn't see the riders pursuing Clark. By now they must have spotted that one of their number was missing.

'You ignored my orders.' He sighed. 'But I'm impressed that you didn't just save your own skin.'

Adna glanced over his shoulder and shrugged.

'Don't be too grateful. Everything happened so fast I didn't have enough time to think about abandoning you.'

Lincoln returned the smile then patted Adna's back.

'Once we reach the river, we might find somewhere to hide.'

Adna nodded. Then he hunched over in the saddle as he rode at a pace that wouldn't strain the horse while still putting distance between them and Stroud.

They'd ridden for another two minutes when the crack of distant gunfire sounded, followed by a sharp volley of shots, then silence.

Neither man needed to comment on what this meant, although Adna encouraged their mount to hurry on through the night. They both avoided looking back as they peered ahead, but the bottom of the long slope along which they were riding was devoid of cover.

They'd ridden for another minute when Lincoln heard a commotion behind them, extinguishing his small hope that they had thrown off their pursuers. Cries went up as Stroud urged his fellow riders to speed up.

This time Lincoln looked back; the riders were 200 yards away and closing quickly.

'Bad?' Adna asked.

'Worse,' Lincoln said.

Adna nodded but he didn't try to speed up and, when Lincoln peered past him, he saw the reason why. A hundred yards further on the ground fell away sharply with only starlit darkness being visible beyond. Lincoln narrowed his eyes, but he failed to discern any details beyond the edge.

He leaned forward, aiming to ask Adna if he knew

where they were when his gaze focused on what he was seeing. What he had taken for stars were ripples reflecting moonlight.

They were approaching the river, and perhaps a chance of finding cover, but that hope receded when they crested the edge of the bank and all that was below was the shoreline.

Water washed against pebbles on a gentle incline, this scene receding away on either side into the gloom. Adna glanced downriver, but then hurried the horse on upriver.

Lincoln started to ask why he was heading towards Skull Bend, the one place where they wouldn't find safety, when Adna pointed at a short promontory sticking out into the water.

'I recognize this place,' he said. 'I know where we can hide and make a stand.'

Sparse trees were clinging hold of life along the shingle and beyond them Lincoln could see nothing but more water and the unpromising river-bank.

'I never thought I'd say this,' he said, patting his back, 'but I'll trust you.'

When he judged that the approaching riders should have come over the bank, Lincoln looked back. To his relief, they weren't visible. He kept looking back, expecting them to appear at any moment, but when they didn't, with every stride onwards Lincoln's hopes grew that they might get lucky.

'Get ready to leap down and follow me,' Adna said. He counted down from three.

On one, he drew back sharply on the reins, then leapt from the saddle.

Lincoln followed. Then, as he didn't know exactly where the hiding-place was, he dallied to slap the horse's rump, urging it to hurry on alongside the river.

He ran after Adna and slipped through the trees. They crested a shingle bank below which was a tangle of debris that had washed up on to the promontory.

Logs lay at angles and among them was a holed and upturned boat. It was five feet long and it had probably been used for fishing or rowing across the river. Although it was a less appealing hiding place than Lincoln had hoped for, he followed Adna in running to the boat.

They slipped down behind the heap of rotten wood. Then they found a rent in the side that let them burrow underneath it.

They both caught their breath as through a hole at the front Lincoln watched their horse skitter along the riverside, kicking up its heels as it showed no signs of stopping before it reached Skull Bend.

Long moments passed, with the wash of water against the boat and pebbles providing the only noise. Then the riders appeared at the top of the bank, emerging a few dozen yards behind the horse.

'They were trying to outflank us,' Lincoln whispered as he watched two riders follow the horse, but sadly Stroud was close enough to see that they were no longer riding it.

Accordingly, Stroud stopped and exhorted the men to desist from their pursuit. He looked back along the riverside.

When his gaze passed the boat, Adna nudged Lincoln and murmured with hope, but when Stroud had looked along the bank to check they hadn't gone in the other direction he looked at the promontory.

His gaze drifted over the logs and sparse trees before it settled on the boat. Then he pointed at them.

'They'll be hiding behind the boat!' he shouted, while waving at the riders to investigate.

'Damn,' Adna murmured as the riders dismounted and advanced on them with steady determination.

'It was a long shot,' Lincoln said, 'but they'll have to get us out of here and we'll make them pay a heavy price.'

'Or we could use the boat as a raft and float away.'

Lincoln dipped a hand into the cold water between his knees and shivered.

'No. We'll be sitting targets while we freeze to death. We stay and fight.'

'You stay. I don't intend to be in the water for long.'

Adna drew Lincoln forward and pointed upriver.

Lincoln tore his gaze away from the gunmen and, with his head pressed to the side of the boat, he saw the bright lights that had interested Adna.

He wondered whether he were seeing the distant town of Skull Bend, but the lights were moving downriver. Then he realized what it was.

A boat was coming towards them.

CHAPTER 10

They'd trapped him.

Daniel peered through the gap in the open door at the small expanse of corridor that was visible to him. Ten feet away and getting closer, the two gun-slingers were kicking open every door in the corridor and looking inside.

Daniel was in the last room, which had been sparsely furnished even when it had been used to berth guests. All that was inside was a bunk set against the wall with a thin straw mattress. The only other feature was a porthole that was too small to get through, but which let him look out on to the riverside, which was darker now that they'd drifted beyond Skull Bend.

Earlier, after Daniel had cut the rope securing the boat to the pier, the sudden lurch out on to the water had knocked him, Samuel, and his men over. In the confusion, Daniel had lost his sword, but he had managed to slip away. The guards had always been a few steps behind him.

They'd concentrated on finding him rather than trying to stop the boat from making its steady way downriver. But after fifteen minutes of searching, the engineers had halted the wheels, leaving the boat to the mercy of the current.

He hadn't seen his brother since his last sighting before he'd cut the ropes. Back then Henry had been struggling to free himself while being dunked in the water on the revolving paddlewheel.

Daniel hoped that when the wheels had stopped Henry had been above water, but it was long past the time when he could help him if he hadn't been.

A clatter sounded as the door to the room beside him was kicked open. One man grunted as he confirmed the room was empty. Then footfalls sounded as the other man moved on to his room.

With only moments to act Daniel grabbed the mattress, brought it up to his chest and turned. He barged into the open doorway as the man moved to come in. They faced each other. Daniel's surprise appearance bought him a few precious seconds, which he used to slam the mattress against the man's chest and push.

He drove him out into the corridor, then carried on shoving until he slammed him into the wall. Daniel reached round the mattress, seeking the man's gun, but the second man was coming out of his room. Daniel swung away and leapt at him.

He caught the man while he was still in the

doorway and pressed him back against the door-jamb. With a frantic motion he grabbed the wrist of his gun hand and moved to wrest the weapon from his grip, but the man swung his arm up higher, forcing Daniel to stretch for it.

With his body exposed, his assailant swung a short-armed jab into Daniel's stomach, making him fold over. Then he struggled, trying to push him away.

Daniel heard the first man kicking himself free of the mattress, so he gave up on trying to reach the gun. Instead, he righted himself and lunged forward, wrapping his arms around his opponent.

He held him tightly to his chest and walked him round until he could see the other man over his shoulder. He rolled his shoulders, gathering his strength.

The delay gave the man the chance to jerk the gun down towards him, but before it reached him, Daniel bundled his opponent away.

The man back-paced twice, but then his foot caught on the edge of the discarded mattress and he went tumbling into the other man. Both of them went down. Before his good fortune ran out, Daniel turned on his heels and ran down the corridor.

It was twenty feet to the corner that led on to a short flight of steps, but it felt ten times longer as, with every frantic pace, Daniel expected a bullet in the back. But he reached the corner without gunfire erupting.

At the run he grabbed the corner and used his momentum to swing himself up the steps. He caught a glimpse of the men gaining their feet and beginning to chase after him. Then he pounded up the steps four at a time and barged the door open with a shoulder.

A man was standing before him on the hurricane deck.

Daniel moved to push him aside, but then he jerked his hand back when he saw that the man was his brother.

'You're in a hurry,' Henry said, smiling.

Daniel looked him up and down, noting the puddle of water around his feet.

'And you're wet, but we haven't got the time to talk.'

Daniel turned away aiming to run along the deck, but Henry grabbed his shoulder, halting him. He pointed upwards. Daniel got his meaning and, as footfalls thudded at the bottom of the steps, he bent and locked his hands together.

Henry stepped into the cradled hands and Daniel gave him a lift up to the Texas deck, where he grabbed the rail and then reached down.

Then, with Henry tugging and with Daniel jumping, Daniel scrambled up to join him. Side by side they stood on the outside of the rail as the first man emerged through the door.

Moving as quietly as they were able, Daniel and Henry swung over the rail. Then they slipped back to get out of view from anyone down below. Thankfully, grunted comments sounded below, questioning which way Daniel had gone.

Footfalls pounded, the sounds splitting up and going in opposite directions. In relief, Daniel peered along the deck. One set of steps was at the front beside the pilothouse with the deck stretching around the centred cabins.

He slipped to the corner on the side where the steps were so that he could look out for the men coming up.

'Staying in the shadows,' Henry said at his shoulder, 'is our best hope.'

'It is.' Daniel sighed and cast him an anxious look. 'I'm sorry about what I did to you. I tried to—'

'Save your breath. We both did the best we could, and your plan was a good one.'

Daniel shrugged. 'I hadn't planned to set us adrift.'

'Planned or not, it's worked well. We've isolated Samuel and we're heading downriver towards Empire Falls.'

Daniel smiled for the first time in a while.

'Our plans to get Samuel back to Empire Falls were shaky, but perhaps we could ride the waters and get him there.'

He had meant his comment to be taken humorously, but Henry nodded thoughtfully as if he'd been considering this very plan for a while.

'Everyone thinks I'm dead, so I've been watching

from the shadows and I reckon if we time it right, we might be able to do just that.'

Daniel flinched, wondering if he were joking, but he accepted that Henry had now regained his usual authoritative demeanour, so he looked around while seriously considering the matter. In the moonlight, the riverbanks presented a stark terrain, showing they'd sailed well beyond Skull Bend and were steering a course in the centre of the river.

The gentle hum from the engine below and the white cloud of smoke from the twin smokestacks that stood before the pilothouse showed that the boat was capable of being piloted. Even though it was adrift, they were moving slowly in the right direction.

'Why haven't they turned back to town?' he asked.

'Samuel works in the shadows. He punishes people on the wheel for show, but most of his debtors are dealt with out of sight. I reckon he's steered away from town so he can kill us quietly.'

'So we'll go downriver until he finds us. But if we can turn the tables on him, we could carry on.'

'That's my thinking. I reckon two men are looking for you and two more stayed with Samuel in the pilothouse. The rest are engineers, so I don't reckon they'll cause us trouble.'

'In that case we need to capture Samuel first.'

Henry winced, acknowledging the difficulties ahead.

'I agree.'

Raised voices sounded below, followed by the heavy thud of footsteps coming up the steps.

Both men slipped back to stay out of view, but the new arrival made straight for the pilothouse. A short debate took place, after which the man went back down the steps. Presently, shouted orders were delivered below.

'Obviously,' Daniel said, 'they can't find us and he's been told to keep searching.'

Henry opened his mouth to reply, but then the hum from below changed pitch. The wheels shuddered. They didn't start turning, but clearly a change of plan was being put into operation. Henry looked around for inspiration.

'We need a change of plan too,' he said. 'And a distraction.'

Daniel murmured that he agreed, and the two men slipped into the shadows to debate their options.

Ten minutes later Daniel sidled along the side of the housing. He kept his back to the wall to stay in the shadows. Ahead was the broken window through which he'd rolled out only an hour ago.

At the window he knelt and listened. From within the pilothouse, the steady creak of the wheel punctuated the silence. As he hadn't seen anyone emerge, he presumed that two men were still with Samuel. So he had to hope that Henry's distraction would urge at least one of them to move away.

This thought reminded him that his task would be easier if he had a weapon. When he looked around, the glints of broken glass on the deck shimmered in the moonlight and drew his attention.

With one eye on the window he shuffled forward and sorted through the glass until he found a lengthy shard. Its base was wide enough to slip into his hand and the end tapered to a sharp edge.

With a kerchief wrapped around his hand, he picked up the shard. It felt comfortable in his grip. If he had to use force, the blunter end would probably cut his palm, but the sharp end would still do more damage to its target.

He waited patiently for Henry to reach the main deck and make his move. Another five minutes had passed quietly when a crash sounded outside the saloon room.

The steps were out of his sight on the other side of the deck, so Daniel slipped under the window to the corner of the pilothouse, where he awaited developments.

'What was that?' Samuel said in the pilothouse.

'Perhaps they've got him,' someone said.

Another loud crash sounded. Then a chair hit the top of the rail, broke, and splayed broken wood along the deck.

'Then help them.'

Daniel smiled as two men ran out of the door with guns brandished and made for the top of the steps. Their footfalls were loud and fast, so Daniel

110

presumed that Henry would now run for safety.

He waited until they'd both disappeared from view. Then doubled over, he ran along beneath the windows at the front of the pilothouse to reach the door.

He paused for breath and rehearsed his next actions in his mind. Then he kicked off from the deck and burst in through the door. The situation inside was as he'd imagined it, with Samuel keeping a casual steadying hand on the wheel while peering through the window.

As Samuel's eyes opened wide in surprise, in two long strides Daniel reached him. He slapped a hand on his shoulder, spun him round to get behind him, and brought the makeshift knife up to his throat.

'I don't want to kill you,' he muttered in his ear. He pressed the glass against Samuel's neck, digging into the flesh. 'So don't force me.'

Samuel stiffened. 'Your brother must have survived the wheel, but with my men after him, he won't be free for long. Is your hatred of me strong enough to let him die?'

'Henry will get away.'

To stop himself having to dwell on this worrying possibility, he pushed Samuel to the door. Outside on the deck he positioned himself facing the steps and awaited developments.

He didn't have to wait for long. Henry came into view, pacing up the steps with his head bowed and his hands raised. A firm shove sent him out on to

111

the deck. Two men followed.

Henry looked up, his stiff posture showing that he was aggrieved at having been captured quickly, but the sight that confronted him made him smile and Samuel's men stomp to a halt.

'So,' Samuel said, 'he didn't escape and we have a stand-off.'

One man slapped a hand on Henry's shoulder and thrust his gun into his captive's side, while the other man walked sideways along the front of the deck to get closer to Daniel and Samuel.

'That's far enough,' Daniel said. 'Another pace and your boss dies.'

The men looked at Samuel for instructions, but he said nothing, waiting for Daniel to make the next move. But Daniel could only gulp, unsure what that move should be.

The guard at the top of the steps cast a significant glance at the other guard, which was returned with a long stare that suggested a silent message had been passed.

Then, with a nonchalant air, the nearer of the men paced onwards with slow, deliberate steps that took him past the pilothouse. To keep him in view, Daniel had to swing round.

A cry of alarm sounded from the other man.

Thinking that whatever plan they'd concocted was coming to fruition, Daniel gripped Samuel around the shoulders and dragged him back to the door. But when he looked towards the steps, it was to see the guard tumbling out of view down them. Henry stood back, watching his progress, his open-mouthed surprise showing he hadn't made him fall.

Long moments passed while everyone stared at the steps. Then a new man rose into view.

Samuel's second man flinched, then swung his gun towards him, but he was too slow and a gunshot to the chest made him stumble against the rail. He toppled over it. A moment later a thud sounded as he hit the hurricane deck, but by then Daniel had recognized the new and unexpected arrival.

'Howdy,' he said, 'Marshal Lincoln Hawk, I'm pleased you've decided to join us.'

CHAPTER 11

'What's the situation?' Lincoln asked.

While Daniel gave him a brief summary, Lincoln checked the Texas deck, confirming that they'd dealt with the immediate danger. Henry was at the top of the steps while his new-found ally Adna stood on the other side of the deck. Both confirmed that the situation was under control.

'If we keep heading downriver,' Daniel said, finishing his explanation, 'we'll reach Empire Falls.'

While wringing out a corner of his jacket to add to the growing puddle at his feet, Lincoln peered at the dark mass of the river. He judged that when he'd seen the boat drifting downriver from the bank it had been travelling faster than a man could walk.

'At this rate that'll be late tomorrow, a long time to keep whoever is still on board at bay, along with the rest.'

'The rest?'

Lincoln updated Daniel and Henry on how he

had come to join them. He and Adna had managed to float the boat out on to the water before Stroud and his men reached them, after which they'd been peppered with lead.

Thankfully, the boat had afforded adequate protection and, as the river bottom sloped away steeply, their pursuers hadn't been prepared to swim out and follow them.

The orders that Marshal Stroud had barked out from the riverbank hadn't indicated too much annoyance; he seemed more excited that this interesting twist had prolonged the chase. Lincoln had floated too far out into the water to hear whether that attitude changed when it became apparent he and Adna were seeking to reach the steamboat.

With that in mind, Lincoln paced up to their captive.

'Tell them about the rest, Samuel,' he said.

Despite the shard of glass at his throat, Samuel considered him with contempt.

'A lawman's got nothing on me.'

'One of your victims has joined me: Adna Burroughs. He was in your debt, so he robbed banks. When he failed to raise the money, you set Stroud on him.' Lincoln waited until Samuel reacted with a slight narrowing of his eyes. 'For sport.'

'Nobody cares about the fate of a failed bank robber.'

'Perhaps, but they sure will care when they find

out that Stroud used me for sport too.'

Samuel gulped. 'I didn't order him to do that.'

Now that he knew he'd worried him, Lincoln smiled.

'We'll let the court in Empire Falls decide, and you'll improve your chances of being believed if you call off your men on this boat, along with Stroud.'

Samuel smirked as he weighed up the situation.

'Go to hell, lawman. You'll never get me to Empire Falls.'

Samuel continued to mutter threats, but Lincoln turned his back on him and walked towards the front of the deck. He kept far enough back from the rail in case anyone below tried to take a pot-shot at him while he assessed the help he might expect from the men at his disposal.

He judged Daniel and Henry to be proficient enough to help, although Adna would probably turn on him if he saw a chance to run. So for his first action he ordered Adna to bring back the body of the man who had fallen over the rail.

Adna did this quickly and he didn't complain when Lincoln took the six-shooter he'd claimed away from him and gave it to Daniel. Lincoln noted this without comment, although when Adna noticed that he was the subject of Lincoln's critical regard he moved away from the others to stand beside the pilothouse.

'You going to arrest me, then?' he asked when Lincoln joined him.

116

'You've been under arrest since I first caught you.'

'But you'd be dead if it wasn't for me.'

'I know, and that'll count in your favour when I hand you over to the court. When you explain the role Samuel Holdstock had in this, it'll count even more.'

'But not enough for me to walk away a free man?'

Lincoln set his hands on his hips and lowered his tone. Adna knew he wouldn't make any promises he couldn't deliver.

'That's not for me to decide, but I doubt it. The choice is yours. Take your fair punishment or cross me and get dealt with as a bank robber.'

'Obliged for your honesty.' Adna took a deep breath. 'But the big question for me is, if I find another weapon, can I keep it?'

'And that's the big question for me too. Find one and bring it to me. Then we'll decide.'

Adna nodded and resumed keeping lookout at the corner of the deck. This time he sat and rested his back against the rails in a position that let him see along the lower decks and the back of the Texas deck.

Henry took the opposite corner, ensuring that they covered both sides of the boat, the only blind spots being beneath them outside the saloon room and behind the other rooms at the stern.

These being the full extent of the precautions they could take, Lincoln took over the duty of guarding Samuel from Daniel. He ordered Daniel to try to get some sleep, so Daniel headed away to Samuel's office.

The long night had begun.

As it turned out, despite Lincoln's concern that someone might make a move on them, the night passed without incident.

Every few hours they changed duties, ensuring that everyone got a short sleep, although come sundown Samuel was the only one who appeared rested, having spent the night sleeping soundly.

Whether the lack of an attack meant that Samuel had exaggerated the number of men who were still on board, Lincoln didn't know, but the daylight raised his and the rest of his group's spirits.

They were steering a steady course down the centre of the river and their steady passage between the banks was fast enough to make Lincoln believe they would reach Empire Falls by sundown.

As Samuel's calm demeanour didn't change, everyone stayed on alert, but the morning passed quietly with no unexpected sounds emerging from the boat; only the steady creak of wood and the wind whistling through the paddlewheels could be heard.

Since the situation seemed to be serene, Lincoln risked splitting his forces by taking Daniel down to the main deck on a foraging mission.

Each man took it in turns to cover the other as they moved down the steps, along the hurricane deck and then down a second set of steps to the saloon room. Unopposed, they were able to explore the hastily abandoned room.

To their delight they collected several plates of untouched food in a tablecloth. Even better, Daniel found where the guards who had been patrolling the dais had kept extra weaponry.

When they returned to the Texas deck they were loaded down with enough firepower, if not the manpower, to defend the boat against an army. They dumped their haul outside the pilothouse and began splitting it up, but before they could become too relaxed, Henry came over sporting a pensive frown.

'I know where we are,' he said, in a sombre tone that alerted Lincoln to the bad news to come.

'Oh?' Lincoln asked.

He stopped considering whether he should give Adna a gun, and looked at the landscape beyond the riverbank. A distinctive hump-backed ridge was swinging into view several miles on, appearing like a huge discarded saddle on the plains.

'That's Dougal's Ridge,' Henry said, pointing. 'Twenty miles out of Empire Falls, a jumble of rocks, switchback passes and caves.'

'Every lowlife who gets run out of Empire Falls holes up there,' Daniel said, 'but I don't see them worrying us out on the river.'

Henry frowned and didn't reply immediately, giving Lincoln time to consider the ridge and then

Samuel, who was standing by the door sporting his usual confident smile.

'Those men aren't the problem,' Lincoln said, looking to Henry for confirmation. 'Stroud will make his move there.'

Samuel looked away quickly, confirming that this was the case before Henry nodded.

'The river skirts around most of the ridge, but for the last half-mile it cuts through a pass. The sides are sheer with overhanging rocks. Anyone planning an ambush can fire at us and we'll need a heap of luck to hit anyone.'

'Then we have an hour to prepare.' Lincoln picked up a six-shooter. He balanced it on his palm and then underhanded it to Adna.

'Obliged,' Adna said, hefting the weapon.

'Don't be,' Lincoln said with a smile. 'You now have to prove you can be trusted by taking on the most dangerous task of all.'

CHAPTER 12

The pass through Dougal's Ridge towered above the steamboat, the sheer sides casting the river into shadow with their brooding presence. As the sides closed in, the water moiled and rocked the boat.

Daniel had often visited this area, but it had always been on the ridge and he'd rarely come close to the pass, judging it to be treacherous.

'Where do you reckon they'll attack?' he asked, peering up through the thin sliver made by the open door.

Henry craned his neck and pointed at an over-hang a hundred yards ahead.

'They could get almost directly above us there.'

Daniel considered the rock. 'And we won't ever get a clear view of them.'

With that sobering comment, the brothers resorted to silence.

They had taken refuge on the steps down to Samuel's office, where they could look up at the pass and hope to take pot-shots at any attackers while having the same level of cover as the attackers had.

The boat was fifty yards from the overhang when a cry went up from somewhere out of their view at the front of the Texas deck.

'Hey!' Adna shouted, his voice echoing. 'Are you there?'

When the echoes had faded away he continued with his demands, voicing short requests.

'Samuel's with me. We've done a deal. But he's injured. He needs your help. These men attacked him. The boat came loose. We're drifting. Everybody else is dead. I'm the only one left. Help us! Help us!'

The last cry echoed for longer than previous ones, as they'd closed on the overhang and the most hemmed in section of the pass.

'You reckon this'll confuse Stroud and stop him attacking?' Henry whispered.

'A lie sounds convincing if it's hidden in a truth,' Daniel said.

The boat continued on their way, with Adna making repeated pleas for someone to help him. His breathless words let Daniel imagine him jumping up and down, waving his arms above his head. He had to admit that this was brave, as the men whom he hoped to hoodwink were the ones who had tried to kill him, but it appeared to be working.

The overhang came closer and then went out of view over their heads before reappearing as they reached the other side. They had now drifted dangerously close to the sheer rocky sides of the pass, but Lincoln in the pilothouse steered them out into the river, presumably while keeping himself hidden.

This act would appear suspicious to anyone who was watching them, but Daniel started to feel that they had misjudged the situation.

'Stroud can't be in the pass,' Henry whispered, as if by speaking quietly he would ensure that this would be the case.

'Agreed. When do you reckon we'll be safe?'

'Probably never, but when we come out of the pass, the river is wide and placid all the way to Empire Falls.'

Daniel nodded. He continued to watch the sheer walls of the pass recede while trying not to let his hopes grow. Adna had now resorted to calling out only the occasional shout for help.

The echoes were no longer sounding when the boat lurched to the side, making both men lose their footing and slip down the steps. With a stuttering series of jerking movements, the boat tipped as they moved, until it was almost square on to the current.

The fast-flowing water surging out of the narrow pass buffeted the boat, making timbers creak even more loudly. In the saloon tables and chairs crashed against the walls.

'Rocks?' Daniel asked.

'I can't see what's ahead,' Henry said. He edged into the open doorway. 'But we're away from the side.'

Henry raised himself. He winced and jerked backwards to sit with his back against the wall.

'Stroud?' Daniel asked.

'Yeah. He's found a boat. Now he's in the middle of the river, waiting for us to come to him.'

Daniel moved to the door and raised himself so that he could see the water through the front rail. He couldn't see the boat until he was standing, as they were closing on it quickly.

The boat was aimed upriver, with two rowers working hard to move it nearer a bank. At first Daniel thought Lincoln was trying to steer the steamboat away so that they would pass by. Then he saw that he was trying to plough into it.

Drifting downriver almost sideways, the steamboat presented a barrier that Stroud would do well to avoid. Accordingly, as the steamboat moved to the left, they rowed in the opposite direction. The closer the two crafts came to each other the more Daniel and Henry moved out to monitor their progress, figuring that they didn't need to keep themselves hidden any longer.

When the boat disappeared from view, the rowers were embarking on a seemingly doomed attempt to miss the bow. Then there came a muffled crash, and raised voices sounded.

With a glance at each other, the two men slipped along the deck to the stern. When they reached the rail, broken wood was drifting by. More pieces came into view as Lincoln tried to straighten the steamboat, but no bodies were amongst the debris.

A gunshot rang out at the bow.

Both men dropped to their knees and stayed down for a moment. Then they risked bobbing up to look along the deck to where Stroud and his men would seek to climb aboard, if they'd survived the crash. But the steamboat's bow was clear.

From the corner of his eye Daniel saw movement. He turned to see two men scurrying into hiding beside the paddlewheel. They were both dry and not close to the position where the boats would have collided.

'Two boats? Or were they already on board?' Daniel asked.

'I reckon they've been holed up all along,' Henry said, 'waiting for Stroud to arrive.'

'Then there's no point in hiding. Come on. Let's make them wish they'd stayed quiet.'

Henry nodded. With their heads down they headed along the deck, seeking to outflank the men who had appeared. But when the other side of the paddlewheel swung into view, to his horror Daniel saw that they weren't facing just two men. Four men were crouched down looking up towards the pilot-house and covering two more men who were making their way to the steps.

Henry took aim at a man who was moving towards the steps while Daniel aimed at another man. They glanced at each other to coordinate their attack. Then they peppered two quick shots apiece. The shots flew wide and kicked splinters from the deck behind the men, but they made them scramble into hiding behind a barrel.

The men by the paddlewheel swung round to face them. Daniel and Henry ducked down. Then they scurried along to get closer to the pilothouse, aiming to gain a different angle on the gunmen. But when they bobbed up the gunmen quickly homed in on them and lead splattered the wall behind them forcing them to dive for cover.

Shots rang out from in front of the pilothouse, showing that Adna and Lincoln were now aware of the attempted assault. Any hope that they'd be able to subdue it fled when further gunfire sounded from the other side of the pilothouse.

Then, before Daniel could think of how they would repel the attackers, a shout went up from the other side of the boat. The voice was authoritative and although Daniel couldn't hear the words, they sounded like orders.

'Surrounded,' Henry murmured unhappily.

Daniel nodded, but he hurried away to check. On reaching the back Stroud and his group had established themselves on the main deck from where they were gesturing to other men out of Daniel's sight.

The hopelessness of the situation made him look at the riverbank, drifting by fifty yards away. As the current was becoming calmer the further they travelled from the pass, swimming to the side would be achievable.

'We need to split up,' Daniel said, pointing. 'Stroud must have left horses near by. You can swim to—'

'I'm not leaving you,' Henry snapped.

'We can't both abandon Lincoln, and if you're free you can get help from Empire Falls to recapture the boat.'

'You should do that. You're the lawman.'

'Not for long, but I left you swinging on that wheel last night. I'll take the bigger risk this time.'

Henry glared at him with a look that said he was prepared to argue until they were overcome, but another burst of gunfire from the bow forced him to lower his head.

'All right,' he whispered. 'But don't get yourself killed over this. If the situation becomes hopeless, surrender and then wait until I can free you.'

Daniel patted his back, then raised himself to consider the perimeter of the boat. The attackers were only in control of small sections and, as Henry's aim was purely to get over the side, he had plenty of choices of where to go.

Quickly they debated the best option. Then Henry hurried along the Texas deck to the back. He peered over the rail and looked at an area of deck on which it was likely that there weren't any people. Then, keeping his head down, he slipped over the rail and crouched down on the other side.

He and Daniel nodded to each other. Then Henry dropped from view. Daniel waited for a few seconds, then jumped to his feet. On the run, he splayed lead at the men below.

He managed three quick shots before they returned fire, after which he dived to the deck. He crawled in the opposite direction for ten feet and jumped up again. From the corner of his eye he saw Henry scurrying along the main deck with his head down, but the distraction of Daniel's gunfire was working, as everybody was peering up at him.

He blasted again while Henry dived over the side. Then he dropped from view.

Several more shots tore out, but they all cannoned into the wall above his head and he heard no shots being fired at anyone else, which gave him hope that nobody had seen Henry's flight.

He shuffled along the deck, moving further away from where Henry had gone overboard. This time he raised a hand and fired blindly. When he reached the corner of the pilothouse, he risked glancing at the water.

Henry's form was receding and falling back as he swam with strong strokes to the riverbank. Then Daniel made his way round to front of the pilothouse, to find Adna lying on his chest facing the steps with his gun thrust out in front of him. Adna flinched when he saw him approach, but he smiled on recognizing him.

'Keep an eye on your side of the deck,' he said. 'I'll cover this side and the steps.'

'Where's Samuel?' Daniel said as he got into position.

'Tied to the pilotwheel.' Adna shrugged. 'He's keeping a reluctant straight course, for now.'

Adna looked around, presumably searching for Henry, while Daniel did the same, wondering where Lincoln was, but before either man could ask, the assault started.

From the stern end below someone hurled up a rope, quickly followed by two more. Daniel trained his gun down the side of the deck and waited for someone to come up, but a man appeared around the side of the last cabin, having reached the Texas deck while remaining out of Daniel's view. He fired two quick shots, then jerked back.

As another man took his place Adna fired down the steps keeping the attackers down until gunfire on his side of the deck forced him to back away.

Gunfire on his side also forced Daniel to move backwards. This let him see Samuel peering through the broken pilothouse window with a casual hand on the wheel and a wide smirk on his face.

Ropes came hurtling up to the rail behind him. Daniel spun round, ready to repel the assault, but he ducked when a shot whistled by his head. He turned to see that two men had slipped along the roofs of the cabins and they were lying facing him on the top of the pilothouse.

He swung his gun up towards them, but before he could aim he saw that Adna was raising his hands in surrender. He darted his gaze to the pilothouse and then to the steps.

Wherever he looked, men were closing in on him. In a matter of moments the situation became hopeless.

Seeing no hope of success, he matched Adna's action by raising his hands. Then Stroud arrived and gestured, making Daniel drop his gun on the deck.

While keeping a gun on them, Stroud hurried to the pilothouse. He probably regretted getting there first when Samuel barked surly orders at him to free him and demanded to know why he'd taken so long.

Two other men came over and beckoned for Adna and Daniel to stand together. As everyone else stayed back, paying more attention to Samuel as he emerged from the pilothouse than to them, Daniel leaned towards Adna.

'We did our best,' he whispered. 'But Lincoln's plan failed.'

'It didn't.' Adna winked. 'That was just the first part, the easy part.'

CHAPTER 13

'Where's Marshal Lincoln Hawk?' Samuel demanded, pacing across the deck to face Daniel and Adna.

'I don't know,' Adna said, raising his chin.

'He was here when we went into the pass. Then he disappeared.' Samuel looked around for Lincoln before he fixed his gaze on Daniel. 'I assume he went into hiding with the other one while you two tried your diversion?'

Daniel had deliberately avoided looking at the riverbank, but he figured that by now Henry would be on dry land and skirting back to the pass in search of Stroud's horses. He put on the most confident smile he could muster and looked Samuel in the eye.

'You're half right,' he said. 'We put up only enough of a fight to stop anyone noticing Lincoln and Henry getting away.'

Daniel swung round to look at the water, then

cast his gaze up to the bank and along it back to the pass. He couldn't see his brother, but Samuel must have got his meaning as he stepped up to him, grabbed his collar, and dragged him up close.

'They ran to save their hides!'

'Nope. They ran to get yours back to Empire Falls and into a court to face the truth, a truth a US marshal now knows and whom you can't silence. When they return they'll have so many men they'll—'

Samuel slapped Daniel's cheek with a back-handed swipe that rocked his head to the side.

As his vision swirled, Daniel looked at the deck. Then, with a shrug, he regained his composure and forced a smile before he raised his head.

Samuel bunched a fist ready to hit him again, but Daniel merely firmed his jaw as he awaited the blow. With a grunt of anger, Samuel converted the move into a turn on his heels to face his men.

'I intend to be in Skull Bend before they get back to Empire Falls. Get the wheels moving and then turn this boat round.'

Two men ran to the steps and disappeared from view. Barked orders ripped out, presumably to the engineers, to carry out his instructions.

'You can't sail upriver fast enough,' Daniel said, 'to avoid Lincoln and Henry.'

'And you won't live for long enough to find out whether you're right.' Samuel gestured for Stroud to take control of them. 'Strap them to the paddle-wheels. We'll see how arrogant they are when we reach Skull Bend.'

The order panicked Adna into running for the nearest rail. He managed only a few paces before two sets of firm hands clamped down on his shoulders and pushed him to his knees. Daniel moved to leap at Samuel, but Stroud grabbed him from behind and held him firmly.

Samuel watched these actions with calm amusement and even walked with them as they were led to the steps.

Their impending fate made both men dig in their heels, forcing their captors to fight to drag them on for every step, but inexorably they were shoved along.

When they reached the top of the steps the two men whom Samuel had dispatched to start the wheels were returning; they were sporting pensive expressions.

'We've got a problem,' one man said.

The two men glanced at each other before the second man delivered the bad news.

'It's the engine. Someone's sabotaged it.'

Lincoln wiped the river water from his face and settled down under the blade. It was at an angle and he felt as if he were in danger of slipping off. But he'd been short of time to find somewhere to hide and the paddlewheel had been the only place he could reach without being seen.

He was lying on a blade beneath the main deck

level and a few feet above the water. The splashing had drenched him, making his hands slick, but he had a good grip of the blade and he reckoned he could hang on until they reached Empire Falls.

That was provided he wasn't discovered. If he was, he'd resolved to dump the rod that was sticking out of his pocket.

He didn't understand how the engine worked, but when the ambush had started and everyone had rushed out, he'd sneaked into the engine room. He'd studied the cranks and rods until he'd found a three-foot length of metal that he could unbolt and which looked important.

This turned out to be so; the paddlewheel had yet to turn and, from the distant cries of alarm, it appeared that he had disabled the engine.

Fifteen minutes passed before he overheard confirmation of what had happened. Two engineers approached the wheel, grumbling to each other, but they fell silent when Samuel's loud voice spoke up.

'How much longer before I can strap them to the wheel?' he demanded, stomping to a halt on the main deck ten yards from Lincoln's hiding-place.

'Not sure,' one engineer said. 'We're—'

'I need an answer. The other two will be coming back and I'm exposed out here.'

Beneath the deck Lincoln smiled with relief that Samuel thought he'd got away with Henry.

'We'll get it working before we reach Empire Falls,' the second engineer said. 'We just need something to replace the pendulum rod.'

'Then do it and fix it back to the. . . .' Samuel trailed off. Then he made up for his lack of knowledge about the workings of the engine with several oath-filled promises about what would happen to them if they failed.

'The longer we stand around here talking,' the first engineer said, his voice becoming truculent, 'the less likely it is we'll fix it in time.'

A sharp intake of breath sounded. 'Get it done. Then I'll find someone else to look after my boat.'

'Do it. The moment I get it working, I'm leaving.'

Heavy footfalls paced away. The second engineer murmured a few placating comments to Samuel. Then he scurried away.

Silence dragged on for a minute until Samuel's shadow loomed over a blade, suggesting he was leaning on the rail and peering at the passing river. Then, with a grunt, he moved away and climbed the steps to the pilothouse.

The next three hours passed quietly. Lincoln gently swayed on the blade while the water glided by a few feet below. He looked out for landmarks, but, although he was familiar with the terrain north of Empire Falls, seeing it from an unfamiliar position made it hard for him to judge how close they were getting.

Occasionally men walked by, but they didn't come close enough for him to hear their conversations. Only Samuel's orders reached him and they became increasingly irritated. Later, the light level dropped without Lincoln catching sight of the town.

Samuel ordered everyone not to provide any light other than that required to repair the engine, so that they could drift by the town unseen. Those orders appeared to be unnecessary when, for the first time since Lincoln had disabled the engine, the paddlewheel lurched and then jerked into motion.

Lincoln grabbed hold of the side, the movement cramping his muscles after spending so much time not moving. Quickly, he planned how he would manoeuvre himself out of his situation. But the wheel stopped and a distant cry of anger sounded.

Lincoln smiled, but his delight was short lived. Five minutes later the wheel moved again, this time with a slower and smoother motion.

Lincoln's head dipped towards the water, and so he took advantage of the night's darkness to lever himself up on to blade above. He repeated the action twice more as the wheel continued to turn at a slow pace.

He wasn't surprised when Samuel came down the steps, barking out instructions with every pace.

'More speed,' he said when he reached the bottom.

'You'll get it,' someone said, 'just as soon as—'

'Enough excuses. We need to beat the current. And those are Empire Falls's lights ahead.'

This comment gave Lincoln renewed hope, but when the wheel speeded up he had no choice but to risk coming out. He clambered up on to the next blade, swung up on to the next, and then, while crouched down, he jumped over to the rail.

He peered around to confirm that nobody was close. Then he clambered over the rail and hurried to the saloon.

With his back to the wall he listened, but other than the creaking wheels and Samuel berating the engineers, he heard nothing. He sidled along the wall to the stern and slipped into the shadows beneath an overhanging stretch of the boiler deck.

By now the wheels were turning smoothly at a steady rate that was strong enough to speed their passage through the water. Faint light was playing across the deck and walls from the approaching Empire Falls, suggesting that this sudden return to working order would let them reach the town within minutes if they didn't turn the boat.

A line of men emerged from a door beside the saloon with Samuel pacing along behind, gesturing. Lincoln considered them, wondering if he could capture Samuel and bundle him overboard now that they were close to town. But he judged that there were too many men with him, and yet others were coming down the steps to check on progress.

'Get back up there and turn this boat round,' Samuel shouted. 'The wheels are working.'

As if in confirmation, the paddlewheels speeded up, splaying water as they ploughed the boat onwards to the town. Outlying buildings beside the water came into sight and then the main bulk of the town around the pier and the Riverview Saloon became visible.

Accepting that he would have to act now or the moment would be lost, Lincoln watched Samuel storm up the steps two at a time with his men surrounding him.

Then he looked up at the boiler deck. He dragged a barrel over and stood on it to reach the bottom of the deck. In short order, he dragged himself up.

He then used the rail to reach the hurricane deck. Above, men were milling around the pilot-house, but they were all looking forward at the town, which was now spreading out before them.

Lincoln scurried to the wall beneath the Texas deck. Then, with a leap, he reached the rail and dragged himself up. Again he slipped into the shadows.

He was on the side facing away from the town and only one man was visible. This man was standing guard twenty paces down the deck, but he was straining his neck to see what the commotion was.

Lincoln made him pay for his lack of attention by sneaking up on him from behind and delivering a sharp chop to the back of his neck, which knocked him into the wall. The man stood swaying and stunned until Lincoln grabbed his shoulders and thudded his forehead against the wall. He collapsed without a sound.

Lincoln looked up to the front of the deck, but the men there were still facing forward. So, keeping in the shadows, Lincoln paced along the deck sideways with his gun drawn and held beside his cheek as he prepared to cause mayhem the moment someone noticed him. But he managed to slip along the deck without anyone reacting.

He'd reached the back of the pilothouse when the boat swung to the side, forcing him towards the rail. This showed that they were turning the boat towards town as they embarked on a manoeuvre that would circle them around in the centre of the river.

The nearer riverbank was only fifty yards away, but gradually the gap opened up. By the time Lincoln had reached the broken window at the side of the pilothouse, Empire Falls was swinging into view as they crossed the river.

He edged forward. Four men were holding Adna and Daniel captive at the front of the deck. Samuel was in the centre, peering ahead with his arms folded, as if defying the town to somehow capture him.

Lincoln leaned forward to look into the pilothouse. Stroud was inside. He was gripping the pilotwheel and leaning to the side as he forced the boat to make the sharpest turn it could manage.

Stealthily, Lincoln placed a hand on the sill. Then he vaulted into the pilothouse.

Stroud reacted slowly, only waving a dismissive

hand in his direction, presumably because he'd been receiving continuous complaints and instructions. Then he jerked away from the wheel, realizing what he'd seen from the corner of his eye, but he was too late.

Lincoln bounded forward and swung a pile-driver of a punch to Stroud's cheek that sent him tumbling across the pilothouse to crash into the back wall. As he slid down it, to lie sprawled and unconscious over the lazy bench, Lincoln grabbed the wheel.

Nobody on the deck was looking at him. The noise from the churning paddlewheels and the creaking of the boat as it battled to run sideways against the current had masked his arrival.

Everybody was looking at the pier 300 yards away. The saloon lights created long shadows behind each of the men who stood like silent sentinels on the deck. Slowly, the shadows tracked sideways as the boat steered round on a route that would make a broad arc before tacking back upriver.

In town, some people were out on the pier watching the unusual sight of a steamboat that hadn't been out on the water for years passing by. They appeared good-natured as they chatted amongst themselves and nobody looked as if they'd act aggressively.

Lincoln kept one hand on the wheel as he considered the men before him. Then he gripped the wheel tightly and swung it in the opposite direction.

Creaks sounded and water buffeted the boat, but

the vessel continued on a course that swung it away from the pier. Lincoln continued to spin the wheel in the opposite direction and slowly his action had the desired effect: the turning stopped.

Then the boat swung back to move towards the pier.

Everybody shuffled forward to the rail, peering at the river and then at the pier and the Riverview Saloon.

Samuel was the first to realize that they were no longer moving round to go upriver. He turned to face the pilothouse, words of anger on his lips, but they died when he saw who was at the wheel.

Lincoln and Samuel stared at each other. Then Samuel raised his right hand to point at him.

'It's Lincoln,' he shouted. 'Get him.'

CHAPTER 14

Daniel had almost given up hope when Samuel's warning cry went up.

He and Adna had been exchanging glances, debating silently whether they should try to make what would probably be a futile assault on Samuel or wait to see whether Henry had gathered reinforcements.

Daniel turned to see Lincoln standing in the pilothouse, one hand on the wheel, a cocked six-shooter in the other.

The guards swirled round to face him, scrambling for their guns, but before any of them could draw Lincoln released the wheel and started firing. He blasted lead with grim efficiency, cutting a swath through the men to Daniel's left.

Man after man went down, each clutching his chest. Then Lincoln ducked as retaliation came from the surviving standing men. Glass shattered as gunfire peppered the pilothouse.

Aside from the two engineers working on the engine, all of Samuel's men were on the Texas deck. This meant that the eight men standing here were his only help.

Daniel resolved to even the odds. With a glance at Adna, who nodded in return, he leapt at the nearest man.

This man was firing at the pilothouse, but when he saw Daniel coming he turned, his gun swinging towards Daniel. Daniel caught the wrist and shoved the gun up.

A single shot tore into the air.

Other men moved to take him on, but Adna leapt at one of the gunslingers whose attention was distracted. He pushed him back against the rail and wrestled for his gun.

Lincoln having meted out destruction from the pilothouse, and Daniel and Adna fighting back, Samuel looked to and fro, weighing up the situation. He delivered his orders.

'You two,' he shouted, 'kill the prisoners. The rest, keep your guns on the pilothouse and shoot the moment Lincoln appears.'

Everyone did as ordered. Two men moved in with guns brandished, looking for an opening to shoot Daniel and Adna, while the other men spread out and took up defensive postures as they waited for Lincoln to risk showing himself.

Daniel continued to struggle as he tried to get a hand on the gun, but he also swung his assailant round to put his body between him and the gunmen.

Unfortunately, this movement placed his back to the rail. With a smirk, his assailant tried to do what Adna was attempting. He drove onward until Daniel's back was to the rail. Then he continued pushing, trying to tip him over.

Daniel's upper body folded over the side, gradually moving down as the man bore down on him. The movement let him see that with Lincoln steering blind, they were now heading for the pier.

Unless someone veered them away, they would hit it. With the wheels turning quickly, the collision would be in another two minutes and at some speed.

The shock must have registered in his eyes as the man also looked at the rapidly approaching pier.

'Samuel,' he shouted, pointing, 'look!'

As Samuel swirled round to face the bow, Daniel took advantage of the distraction to redouble his efforts in trying to push his opponent away. He braced his back against the rail and then raised himself until he stood upright.

'Shut the engine off,' Samuel shouted.

Over his assailant's shoulder, Daniel saw three men hurry off to do his bidding. After another glance at the pier, Samuel followed them to the steps.

Daniel put him from his mind and thrust up his left hand to grab his assailant's gun hand. With both hands wrapped around the other's wrist, he drew the arm down.

The man shoved him with his shoulder, aiming to barge him over the side, but Daniel absorbed the blow by rocking his weight on to his right leg and then continuing the motion on.

They turned on the spot, the gun still waving widely, but gradually lowering. Their grip of the weapon squeezed out a shot that flew across the deck.

A cry of pain went up as the wild shot found a target. Then Daniel managed to swing the man's gun hand down until the gun was aimed at the deck. This forced Daniel to stand hunched over.

Seizing his opportunity while Daniel was in an awkward position, the man shoved him with his chest and bore down, seeking to knock him down to the deck.

The relentless pressure on his back was too great and Daniel fell to his knees.

The sudden movement made the man stumble over him, to lie on his back. That gave Daniel his chance. He released his grip of the man's wrist, slapped both hands to the deck to steady himself, and then thrust up while twisting.

He lifted the man bodily off the deck. Then, with a deft sideways movement, he tossed him to the side, making him go tumbling.

The man lunged for the rail. His fingers caught it and held for a moment. Then he fell over the side and dropped from view. Best of all, his attempted grab made him release the gun and it went skittering to the deck at Daniel's feet.

Daniel wasted no time in slapping a hand on the weapon. Then he swirled round and put his back to the rail while he surveyed the scene.

Adna had wrestled his opponent to the deck and was hitting him. The deck was clear except for the three men sneaking up on the pilothouse, although they were peering worriedly over their shoulders at the pier, now 200 yards away.

Daniel ran to Adna, who looked up, smiled on seeing he was free, then gathered up the gun from his dazed opponent.

They faced the pilothouse as one man sneaked up to the door. Then, while crouched down, that man thrust his hand through the window. He fired indiscriminately, but he managed only two shots before Daniel dispatched him with a shot that made the man arch his back and stumble to the side.

The other two men turned to see Adna and Daniel break into a run towards them. They wavered before they straightened and burst in through the door.

Adna and Daniel hurried them on their way with gunfire, but both their shots clattered into the swinging door.

Within the pilothouse both men fired on the run, until the first attacker folded over, clutching a belly wound. He walked into the window and fell over the sill, coming to rest with his arms dangling.

The other man carried on moving as Lincoln came into view, rising from behind the wheel. The two men tussled.

A few moments later Daniel reached the door and swung round the jamb to face the wheel. Lincoln and his opponent were slugging it out while the wheel spun out of control.

Daniel moved to help Lincoln as a gunshot sounded, echoing in the confined space.

Then he found that his help wasn't required as the man fell to the floor, his chest bloodied. Lincoln straightened his stance and calmly holstered his gun. Then he stepped over the body to join them.

'Glad to see you stopped enjoying yourself out on the deck,' he said, smiling.

Daniel nodded and turned to check that Adna had slipped in unscathed, but Adna was staring through the window, his mouth wide open with shock. Daniel did a double take when he remembered the other danger they faced.

'Not glad to see you got bored steering the boat,' he murmured.

Lincoln's gaze followed Daniel's, both men looking ahead. Samuel had yet to turn off the engine and they were a hundred yards from the riverside.

They were proceeding on a course which, after Lincoln had released the wheel, would hammer the boat into the pier at an oblique angle.

People were scurrying about on the pier as they fled from the impending collision. Some were running into the Riverview Saloon for safety, while others were running out of it.

Daniel slapped a hand on the wheel, halting it, then swung it round in the opposite direction.

'I'd been aiming to run alongside the pier,' Lincoln said at his shoulder.

Lincoln put a hand on the wheel aiming to direct the boat back to a safer tack, but Daniel shrugged him off.

'I'm not,' Daniel said. He watched the saloon swing back into the centre of the window as he steered a straight course. 'Samuel has controlled the Riverview Saloon from afar for long enough. It's time we let him pay it a visit.'

He glanced at Lincoln, who raised an eyebrow.

'Now that's an interesting plan,' he said. He raised his hand from the wheel. 'I hope Samuel is still out on the deck to watch this.'

Daniel glanced at Adna to check that he knew what would happen next. Adna responded with a shrug and a blowing out of his cheeks.

Then Daniel rolled his shoulders, planted two firm hands on the wheel and faced the pier and saloon, now less than half the length of the boat away.

'This is madness,' a groggy voice murmured behind him. 'You'll all die.'

From the corner of his eye Daniel saw Marshal

Stroud get up off the lazy bench to view the scene ahead while rubbing his head.

A few moments later, the pounding of the wheels on both sides of the boat lessened. Then the hum of the engine became less shrill.

But Samuel had turned off the engine too late.

With a muttered oath Stroud scurried to the broken side window and threw himself out. Nobody moved to stop him. There was no stopping the boat now.

'I said I'd bring you back to Empire Falls, Samuel,' Daniel said. 'And I have.'

Then the boat ploughed into the pier.

CHAPTER 15

Metal crunched and wood snapped as the steam-boat hammered onwards.

The collision made Daniel fall against the wheel while both Lincoln and Adna went sprawling. Daniel clung on as the boat's momentum cut its bow through the wooden pier, slicing between the timbers with the sureness of a knife.

With a crunch the boat hit a strut that was supporting the pier, which made the structure fold like a playing-card trying to withstand a fist.

Clutching hold of the wheel, Daniel was pleased to see that the townsfolk were fleeing in all directions. He reckoned the slowing boat was unlikely to reach them.

Timbers screeched as if in pain and heavy thuds sounded on either side as the wider section of the boat mowed its relentless way onwards. This sent another jolt juddering through the decks. Daniel was again thrown forward and this time he lost his grip of the wheel.

He tumbled over it, landed on his side on the sill, and then went flying through the window. At the last moment he tucked in a shoulder and turned his ungainly descent to the deck into a roll. But with the boat slowing with every yard that it cleaved through the pier, he still went rolling along the deck.

He fetched up against the rail where in desperation he grabbed a tight hold of the struts. He clung on with his head squashed between two struts and his legs splayed with one foot on top of the rail and the other on the deck.

His awkward position let him look along the length of the boat to see that it was listing badly, with the main deck tilting upwards as it ploughed through the pier.

The smokestacks toppled in opposite directions, to land on the boiler deck in an explosion of soot. The left-hand paddlewheel sloughed away while the right-hand one was squeezed upwards before it toppled and fell into the saloon.

Then, with a shudder like an earthquake and a final thundering crash, the boat came to a halt. Daniel tumbled away from the rail, landing on the deck where he lay, holding his breath. With what sounded like a relieved sigh, the boat settled down.

Tentatively Daniel flexed his limbs. He found that they moved so he got to his feet.

His legs shook and he grabbed hold of the rail to steady himself. He considered the damage.

Thuds and crashes were sounding as the settling continued. The pier was on either side of the boat with only the stern end sticking out into the water.

Adna and Lincoln emerged from the pilothouse. On their faces were manic grins, that showed they too hadn't expected to survive the crash. Daniel gave them a thumbs-up signal, then turned to look ahead. He flinched back for a pace, finding to his surprise that he was in the Riverview Saloon.

The bow had ploughed into the saloon's front wall and brought it down, leaving the main deck flattened beneath debris. Daniel therefore stood where the wall had once been, looking down into the main room where a few days ago the townsfolk had gathered for his father's funeral.

Fortunately, the room had been deserted; the few people who were emerging out of hiding were doing so from the main road beyond the saloon.

Daniel turned to search along the boat for a way off. He saw movement.

Samuel Holdstock and Marshal Stroud were tentatively picking out paths along the remnants of the main deck. They were peering at the gap where the paddlewheel had been while searching for the best place to jump on to the rickety pier.

Daniel gestured to Lincoln and Adna, and then to the main deck. Both men moved towards the rail, but his motion attracted Samuel's attention.

From fifty feet apart the two men glared at each other. Samuel was the first to move, when he ordered Stroud to shoot Daniel.

Daniel dived to the deck as slugs whined over-head. Adna and Lincoln stayed down too. When a few seconds had passed and no more gunfire had sounded, Daniel raised his head to see that Samuel had used the distraction to clamber over the side of the boat and on to the pier.

Stroud was following him while keeping his gun aimed backwards. Lincoln broke into a run and, with fearless speed, he ran down the steps three at a time.

As Stroud fired at Lincoln, Daniel moved to follow him, but the impact had weakened the decking and when he kicked off, the deck gave way with a dull crack, leaving a yawning gap. He went down full length, then struggled to gain his feet.

Tentatively, he sidled backwards to the rail and used it to lever himself up. There was a route around the collapsed deck that would get him to the steps, but by the time he reached them, he would be a long way behind Lincoln, who was already jumping down on to the pier.

So he watched Samuel and Stroud run into the wrecked saloon. Standing before them was Wesley Truscott, the owner of the saloon and the man in Empire Falls who was apparently on Samuel's payroll.

Daniel judged that by the time Lincoln reached the saloon, Samuel would have regrouped. With Wesley's help, he and Stroud might be able to make a stand.

Daniel slipped over the rail and jumped down on to the debris below. The broken wood shifted beneath his feet, throwing him to his knees, and it took him precious moments to find a route, but when he set off the mass of broken wood hid him. So he was able to slip beneath the tattered and dangling roof and into the saloon unseen.

He jumped down on to the solid floor, landing among a tangle of knocked-over tables and chairs, from where he heard Samuel barking out orders.

'It's time you showed me why I pay you,' he shouted. 'Get me out of here.'

'I'm delighted I can help,' Wesley said with his usual genial-host demeanour, 'but we may have a problem.'

'I don't care about your problems. This place can be rebuilt, but only if you get me back to Skull Bend.'

Daniel pushed chairs aside to reach clear space. When he came out from round the front of the debris, he saw that Wesley's problem wasn't his wrecked saloon.

Two men were emerging from the back of the saloon: his brother Henry and Ronald Kearny, the man whom Lincoln had put forward as the next marshal of Empire Falls.

Samuel took one look at them and at Wesley's apologetic expression, which said that Wesley wasn't going to help him. Then Samuel drew his gun and blasted a low shot into Wesley's guts that made him fold over and tumble to the floor.

Samuel beckoned Stroud to follow as he hurried behind the bar, presumably with the intention of slipping out through a door to a backroom. On the run, the two men sprayed lead, forcing Henry and Ronald to dive for cover.

Then Daniel saw Lincoln slipping into the saloon; a moment later Stroud saw him too. A few paces away from the bar Stroud skidded to a halt and swung round to face the front of the saloon with his gun held low.

He crouched, but he didn't get to fire. Lincoln's two rapid shots blasted into his chest, making him stagger backwards for a pace. His gun fell to the floor as he toppled.

As Lincoln moved on, his smoking gun thrust out, Samuel scurried behind the bar. He bent forward, his gun picking out Lincoln, but before he could fire Daniel got him in his sights.

Lead tore into Samuel's shoulder, sending him tumbling backwards into the wall behind him while his gun arm jerked up and blasted a shot into the ruined ceiling. He cried out as he fell.

Daniel steadily walked towards the bar as the others moved onwards, cutting off Samuel's escape routes.

'Samuel,' Daniel said, 'I said I'd bring you to Empire Falls to face justice.'

'This doesn't end here,' Samuel shouted from behind the bar. 'You'll never prove anything.'

'We have Adna,' Lincoln said. 'He knows what you did. And we saw you shoot up Wesley Truscott, Empire Falls's most respected citizen.'

'Wesley Truscott!' Samuel snorted a laugh that acknowledged the irony of the situation. 'All right. I'll give myself up and let my lawyers free me.'

A gun clattered on to the bar and then skidded over it to drop on the other side. Then Samuel bobbed up with a smirk on his lips. He held one hand at shoulder level, from where the wounded arm hung dangling.

'I look forward to seeing you fail,' Daniel said, lowering his gun. 'The good people of Empire Falls will learn the truth about what you've done.'

'The truth about Wesley might make things look bad for me,' Samuel said, casting a sneering glance at Wesley's body. 'But the truth about your father will make things even worse for you.'

With that defiant statement, Samuel moved to come out from behind the bar while fingering his wound.

Daniel sought out Henry's attention and nodded, receiving a shrug in return that acknowledged that Samuel might be right. The truth that they'd worked so hard to uncover might prove to be the worst result of all.

From the corner of his eye Daniel saw movement. Gunfire roared. Daniel jerked around as hot fire blasted into Samuel's chest, sending him reeling.

Daniel raised his own gun, but then he saw the

smoke rising from Lincoln's gun as Samuel's hand dropped away from his jacket pocket, although whether he'd been reaching for a concealed weapon, Daniel couldn't tell. Neither did he care.

Samuel sprawled over the bar. His weakening hands clutched hold of the wood for a moment before they opened. Then he slid from view.

'Everyone see the gun he was going for?' Lincoln asked.

'Sure,' Daniel said as Henry and the others murmured their support.

Lincoln stepped up to the bar and peered over it. He frowned.

'It'd seem we won't get to hear what he had to say about Marshal Ellis Moore, after all.'

CHAPTER 16

'You don't want to be the marshal of Empire Falls, then?' Henry asked.

Ronald Kearny glanced down the road, taking in the wrecked Riverview Saloon, which had yet to decide whether it would fall into the road or into the river.

'Nope,' Ronald said with a smile on his lips. 'There's not much left here to be marshal of.'

Daniel joined him and Henry in smiling.

'The town will cope now that it's free of Samuel Holdstock's influence,' he said, 'so I have no problem with you staying. After what you did, I reckon you've allayed Lincoln's fears.'

Both men looked at Lincoln, who had been negotiating for a horse at the stables. He came over and, although he had been too far away to hear their debate, one look at Daniel and Ronald engaged in calm conversation made him nod.

'You did well,' he said. 'I doubted anyone could get Samuel out of Skull Bend. But you found a way.'

'And that's why I can't be the new marshal. I broke every rule in the book to bring him to justice.'

'You did,' Lincoln said, casting an amused glance at Ronald. 'And as soon as you get the strange notion out of your head that that's a problem, you'll do Empire Falls proud.'

Ronald and Lincoln both laughed. Then they headed to their horses. When they'd mounted up, Daniel joined them, still feeling bemused that what he'd thought was his last act as a deputy lawman had probably turned out to be his first as town marshal.

'Aren't you staying to tie up the loose ends?' he asked.

'Nope,' Lincoln said, looking ahead. 'Some of Samuel's men scurried into hiding. They'll pick over the scraps, but you can deal with them.'

'And Adna? I haven't seen him recently.'

Lincoln shrugged. 'He'll hand himself in, though we'll hope not before your other problem goes away.'

'How will. . . ?' Daniel trailed off when he gathered Lincoln's meaning. 'I guess once you've been hunted, you're minded to become a hunter.'

'Sure.' Lincoln leaned from the saddle. 'But if he hasn't turned up in a month, tell me.'

'I'll do that.'

Lincoln raised the reins to move on, then he lowered them and looked at Daniel and Henry.

'You two finished the hard work that Ellis started,' he said. Then he rode on with Ronald trailing along behind.

Daniel and Henry came together to watch them leave. When the riders had moved beyond the edge of town, they considered the damage they'd caused.

The Riverview Saloon was collapsing steadily without anyone's help, the pier had tilted over, and the steamboat lay half-sunk in the water. The towns-folk were edging closer to survey the damage.

'Maybe,' Daniel said with a rueful smile, 'the really hard work starts now.'